F
WAR

Ware, Cheryl.

Venola in love.

$16.99

000035365
05/14/2001

| DATE | | | |
|---|---|---|---|
| | | | |
| | | | |
| | | | |
| | | | |
| | | | |
| | | | |
| | | | |
| | | | |
| | | | |
| | | | |
| | | | |
| | | | |

.1 — 1899

# Venola in Love

by Cheryl Ware

illustrated by Kristin Sorra

ORCHARD BOOKS
New York

Also by Cheryl Ware

*Flea Circus Summer*
*Catty-Cornered*

Orchard Books
95 Madison Avenue, New York, NY 10016

Manufactured in the United States of America
Book design by Rosanne Kakos-Main
The text of this book is set in 12 point Usherwood Book.
The illustrations are pen and ink.

1  3  5  7  9  10  8  6  4  2

Library of Congress Cataloging-in-Publication Data
Ware, Cheryl.
Venola in love / by Cheryl Ware ; illustrated by Kristin Sorra.
p. cm.
Summary: In a series of diary entries and E-mail letters, Venola
describes how her boring year in seventh grade turned
exciting after the arrival of a handsome new student.
ISBN 0-531-30306-3 (trade : alk. paper)
ISBN 0-531-33306-X (library : alk. paper)
[1. Schools—Fiction. 2. Diaries—Fiction. 3. Electronic mail
messages—Fiction. 4. Letters—Fiction.]
I. Sorra, Kristin, ill. II. Title.
PZ7.W2176 Vf 2000 [Fic]—dc21 00-25141

*For Barbie and Rebecca, who make me laugh!*
*Thanks to Ashley, Brooke, Casey, Chaffee, Clarissa,*
*Kate, Laura, Lauren, and Tara.*

*—C. W.*

Dear Diary,

This is the super secret locked-up diary of Venola
Mae Cutright bought with two weeks' hard-earned
paper route profits. I promise to carry you with me
in my backpack at all times and to protect you from
prying eyes as I capture all the most exciting and
heart-wrenching moments of the second half of
my seventh-grade year. PLEASE let there be some
exciting or heart-wrenching moments because if I
wasted my money on you with your stylish yellow
and blue stars and moons, cloth cover, and extra-
strong lock, instead of a pair of jeans like Sally's,
and then nothing exciting happens to write about,
I'll just die. I mean it. Die.

Dear Diary,

Maybe I shouldn't have written in you until some-thing exciting happened because now I'm stuck with you, and out $15.99 plus tax. Wonder if I could cut the first two pages out of you with my X-Acto knife and try to return you? I would probably end up feeling guilty and have to turn myself in, and I'd go to jail, and not have a journal to write in while I'm in the big house. Then my head would explode with all the things I should be writing. Might just be easier and safer to keep you.

Biggest thing that happened today was Mrs. Proudfoot had a big purple vein pop out on her forehead when she was yelling at our class for being "exceptionally unruly." She assigned extra math problems for homework because of our "obvious disrespect for authority and the mathematical school of thought." She gave Sammy Potter detention hall for being "the ringleader." Whoopee. I guess this is nothing new and not even worth writing about, huh? All Sammy does is fold up his eyelids and stuff to entertain us. I wonder if his attempts at humor will cause permanent eye damage. What a dope.

Dear Diary,

This holiday should be abolished! Why should we waste a holiday on ugly little cupids running around with arrows and people being all mushy? Maybe we should have an extra holiday like Halloween, where you get to scare people and eat too much candy, or like Christmas, where people pile presents under a huge tree!

Even when I was in elementary school, Valentine's Day was always the worst day at school because you found out just how unpopular you really were. First, you had to buy those paper valentines and decide which ones to give to your real friends, and then you had to decide whether to give the pretty ones to the popular kids so that they would like you better, and whether to give the ugly ones to people you didn't really like at all. You HAD to give everybody one because if you didn't, the next year you might not get very many in return. People remember things like being slighted on Valentine's Day.

Then just when we get old enough not to have to pass out valentines, the student council thinks up a lousy Valentine's Day fund-raiser. This morning, for fifty cents, you could buy a carnation to be delivered to your sweetheart's homeroom. Gross.

Well, I wasn't expecting one because I don't have or want a sweetheart, so when this ninth grader called out my name, my face turned red, and I went up and got it, thinking it was probably from my friend Sally. But instead it said "ANONYMOUS."

So I started fantasizing about who could have sent it. I was looking around my classrooms—until lunch when three-carnation Sally burst my bubble and said that she had heard "through the grapevine" that Mrs. Knox had bought one for all the kids in her homeroom who weren't getting a flower delivered, and she had them signed ANONYMOUS.

So here I am, a Valentine's Day charity case. Could I be any more depressed?

Mansion Apartment Shack House

Curtis Demsey
A. J. Smith
Jonathan Cruthers

Kyle Jeffries

Jeep Cherokee
Cadillac
Corvette

Mini - van

One child   Twins   Dozen   Five

Monday, March 6

First Period

Dear Diary,

Finally something I deem worthy of writing inside
your exquisitely bound, outrageously expensive
pages! I might just have a seventh-grade life after all.

It all started this morning in homeroom with
a stupid game of MASH. You know, Mansion-
Apartment-Shack-House, the game where you pick
a number like three and count around the MASH
square, crossing out every third option. You keep

crossing things out until you only have one option left on each side of the square, and then you find out who you will marry, how many kids you will have, what kind of car you'll drive, what kind of house you'll live in, and important stuff like that.

I had already decided that I wasn't going to fall in love and act all silly. My girlfriends have been dropping like flies to the disease. It makes them act like they have lost at least 20 IQ points, and the boys in my class aren't much better off. (Not that the boys around here have very high IQs to start with! All they know about is sports and disgusting gross things like collecting baseball cards, hunting, and NASCAR.)

Well, I just knew with the poor selection of male specimens available in Belington, that if I concentrated on other things, this love sickness wouldn't happen to me. Wrong. Here's what happened:

"You're next, Venola Mae. Everyone <u>has</u> to do it," said my best friend, Sally, smiling like a Cheshire cat because her future with a ninth-grade hunk had just been cast in stone (or at least on paper). "Just don't bother listing Jonathan Cruthers as one of your possible husbands because the fates have already arranged for the two of us to spend eternity happily ever after together."

According to the most recent MASH reading,

Sally and Jonathan were going to get married, buy a minivan, and spend the rest of their lives living in a mansion with their one dozen kids. Even if she were living in a mansion, I didn't think that Sally had much to be smiling about with a dozen kids running around. And if anyone should know, it's me because I have four brothers and a sister and deal with life in a large family on a daily basis. And believe me, my mother doesn't walk around with a 24-hour-a-day smile plastered on her face. It's more like a frazzled-dazed-confused look. Dad's facial expression isn't much better, but maybe a little happier because he gets to go out to work during the day and talk to regular people instead of just us.

"I hope a butler and chauffeur come with that mansion, Sally, or you'll never have time to do fun things," I said.

"I'll be too busy for fun, silly. I'm going to be married and have a dozen kids," Sally said, graciously accepting her destiny.

I didn't want to play Sally's ridiculous baby game because, first, I don't believe MASH has ever predicted a single successful marriage, and even more importantly, because I don't have any intentions of settling down until I'm at least in my sixties and have seen the world and accomplished all my goals such as learning to rock climb, to scuba dive peacefully with sharks, and to play the bongos with aborigines in some far, far distant land from Belington. But Sally forced me into it with her best pout/stare. So for future husbands, I halfheartedly chose mostly actors from TV and movies and one rock singer.

"Doesn't count," she said. "They have to be real people who would <u>actually</u> consider marrying you," which was the same as saying I didn't have a chance in a million years of snagging one of the jet-setters from the Hollywood teen scene.

I didn't have the heart to tell her that I had as good a chance with Leonardo DiCaprio as she had with Jonathan Cruthers because Jonathan doesn't even know she is alive and only hangs out with the most popular girls in his own grade. It was too early in the morning to argue, so I held my tongue, erased my superstars, and thought MUCH smaller.

All the guys around here are childish and boring, but I picked A.J. because everyone just expects you to pick A.J. He's the most popular and athletic boy in seventh grade, and he's always breaking up and going with different girls, including both Sally and Missy.

Then I picked Sammy Potter because even though he gets in trouble a lot, he was nice enough to let me copy his algebra equations on the bus this morning. (I could have done them myself, but my love for TV movies overcame my love for math last night.) Anyway, Sammy's superb math abilities might come in handy at balancing our future joint checking account or doing our taxes or something. I might as well be practical if I'm forced to MASH.

After these two guys, I drew a blank. Honestly, I just don't care that much about boys and getting married and dating and stuff.

"Hurry up, Venola, before Mrs. Knox starts taking roll," Sally whined.

Sally's tone was starting to grate on my nerves because, like I said, I didn't get as much sleep as I should have the night before. "Forget it, Sally," I said, "I'm not going to rush into a lifetime commitment of marriage with any ol' slob just because Mrs. Knox is in a hurry to take roll. I can't help it if I'm pickier than you."

Sally didn't even blink at my jab. "Fine, I'll help you. The next two guys to enter through that door are going down as prospective husbands," she snapped.

"Gee," I said, "I wonder if this is how girls in countries with arranged marriages feel."

But she wasn't paying any attention to me. She had her hawk eyes fixed on the door, and my impending nuptials.

Wouldn't you know it, the first gorilla to clomp through the door was Tommy Flint, whose claim to fame is doing disgusting things like gluing his fingers together in art class and then eating them apart, and making fake snot for his science project which I'm not convinced was totally fake. The consistency was way too real.

But then, to my utter surprise, the most gorgeous being on this side of heaven walked through the door. A stranger, complete with the fairy-tale traits of tall, dark, and handsome. Mmmm.

All our mouths fell open and silent, even Sally's for a second or two, while Mr. Perfect walked across to Mrs. Knox, smiled a charming Colgate smile, and handed her the note from the office.

"Welcome, Nathan, I'm sure you'll like it at Belington Junior High. I think you'll find the students nice enough and the academics top-notch," she said, and I knew it was my lucky day. I added "Nathan" in big letters to my list of suitors. Finally, someone different and exciting and NOT Sammy Potter and NOT Tommy Flint has stepped into my world.

Hang on, Diary. You might not be lonely in my backpack if things continue. I might just fill you up and have to moonlight to buy one of your brothers or sisters for Volume II. Gotta go. First period bell is ringing.

Sally,
Do you think Nathan
is as gorgeous as I
do? I think he smiled
at me! Ask him
where he is from.
V.

S.,
Yes, I am nosy, but
you want to know
too!!! If you are too
big of a chicken, get
Sammy to ask him. I
just have to know!
V.

Second Period

Dear Diary,

Thanks to the fine art of note passing and whispering behind the teacher's back, I already know Nathan's last name is Racin and that he and his family just moved to Belington from some strange place called Gallipolis, Ohio, wherever that may be.

Stay tuned! Venola Mae, private eye, is on the loose.

Sally,
Do you think I should invite Nathan to sit with us at lunch?
V.

S.,
You really think it is too soon? I don't want him to think I'm some kind of stalker. I just want to meet him!!!
V.

S.,
Yes, I UNDERSTAND I need to put dibs on him before someone else does! With a face like that, he's not going to be lonely for long!! Could someone as cute as he is like someone like me?
V.

S.,
What do you MEAN
it would take some-
one new who doesn't
know my annoying
ways? Am I REALLY
that annoying?
V.

Ha! Ha! Very funny!
Forgot to laugh!
V.

Study Hall

Dear Diary,

At our school, all the seventh graders are in one
class, so I have the luxury of admiring Nathan from
not so afar, except in third-period English when he
sat directly behind me, so I couldn't watch him the
entire time. I turned around and sneaked peeks at
him as often as I could without appearing completely
obvious. I just pretended I kept needing to look at
the huge calendar on the wall above his head.
Finally Mrs. Knox came over and wrote the date at
the top of my paper with her mean red pen and
underlined it twice.

I'm not sure Nathan even knew I was alive, or
noticed my obsession with the date. But in math
class, I think he smiled at me and blushed when he
picked up my pencil that I dropped by mistake as I
walked past his desk on my way to the sharpener
for the third time. I wouldn't have dropped it in
the first place if Mrs. Proudfoot hadn't screamed,
"Venola Mae Cutright, I'm going to break more than
your pencil lead if you get out of your seat one
more time today. Do you have ants in your pants?"

That's why I'm not sure whether Nathan was smiling at me when he picked up my pencil or laughing at me for getting yelled at by grouchy old Mrs. Proudfoot. What a bear. You'd think she'd want me to have sharp lead to do the bazillion problems she assigns each day to keep us quiet and out of her hair. Teachers can put a real damper on your love life.

I'm not sure how to read Nathan yet. Being new and all, he mostly keeps his head down, working on the dumb math equations like we're supposed to do. The rest of us spend most of the class passing notes and playing practical jokes on each other. I don't think anyone has had the chance to tell Nathan that you don't have to worry too much about doing the actual figuring and coming up with the correct answers because Mrs. Proudfoot never collects the problems we do. She always writes the answers on the board so we can check our "progress" at the end of class.

But today I concentrated even less on math than ever before. That one "maybe-for-me" smile/blush was enough to convince me that I, Venola Mae Cutright, feminist extraordinaire, am uncontrollably and forever head over heels in love with Nathan Racin from the distant shores of Gallipolis, Ohio.

P.S. Sometimes I'm not sure how to take Sally. She said that it would make me more popular if someone as cute as Nathan were to go out "with someone like me." What does that mean? "Someone like me"? Am I an alien or something? Sometimes she makes me feel like a real goon.

Dear Diary,

MY MOM IS THE COOLEST MOM ON EARTH!!!

Guess what? I'm getting a computer! Well, not just me—the whole family. But who cares? Just so we get it. Today she received a killer phone bill which had some major long-distance talk sessions with her sisters. She says she can E-mail all three sisters daily, cheaper than one phone call per month to each of them. So since Mama is mad at the phone company, I WIN! We're going on the Internet!

I tried to call Sally to tell her the good news, but her phone line is busy. She's probably on-line right now. Ever since she got E-mail last month, her number is always busy, but now I can E-mail her!

P.S. I won't forget you, Diary. I can write enough to keep you and a computer happy (even tired!).

18

Home Sweet 'N' Sour Home

Dear Diary,

I never once thought a brother of mine would ever do anything nice for me, especially Melvin, who's a junior in high school and never does anything nice for anyone and who barely notices I exist unless he's trying to get rid of me.

Obviously, today was no different in his eyes. "Get lost, squirt. Watch that obnoxious head-banging music show in your own room. We've got to study for tomorrow's chemistry exam," he growled, and switched the TV to the country music channel while pushing things aside on the coffee table to make room for his and his friend's books.

Here he stood with the most beautiful girl I've ever seen in my whole twelve-and-a-half-year-old life—delicate features, milky translucent skin, big white, straight teeth, bright emerald green eyes, and the most amazing mane of fiery red hair. And Melvin actually thought I was going to believe his mind was on studying the finer points of chemistry.

"I was here first," I said and changed the channel back to MTV. "Go work at the kitchen table," I suggested innocently, knowing full well that Mama was in there cooking supper, would enjoy the company, and would not give Melvin and his new woman a minute's peace. Tee hee.

My specialty since birth has been torturing brothers and their dates, and today was to be no exception. My techniques are much more intricate and subtle than those of my elementary school years, when all I did was put the brother and his date together in a song about "sitting in a tree k-i-s-s-i-n-g" and pushing a baby carriage.

The beauty queen laughed and smacked Melvin lightly on the arm. She turned, handed me her CD Walkman, and slipped the headset around my neck. "If you want to, you can take some of my latest CDs into your room and listen to them for a while. I promise not a one of them is country," she said, rolling her eyes to show me her distaste for country music and to conspire with me about how disgusting my brother Melvin's taste in music is. Then she gave me a smile that would melt Alaska.

It wasn't until an hour and two alternative rock CDs later that I figured out she had gotten rid of me as slick as a whistle without even hurting my feelings. I figure this is a girl I can learn a lot from.

Oh yeah, it wasn't until Gwen (that's her name) left and Mom's endless questioning stopped that I made the connection between this raving beauty named Gwendolyn and my own secret crush. Nathan has a sister, and for some unknown reason, she has been tossed into my path and onto my living room couch, and for some even stranger reason, is attracted to Melvin, the egghead. (Go figure.)

I guess no one can have it all, and Gwendolyn definitely received a double helping of looks, so maybe she was passed over for taste in boyfriends. But I'll straighten her out about all of Melvin's bad points when given the chance. For now, it will be nice to have the sister of the man of my dreams around to pump for information.

P.S. I hope Gwen starts hanging around here a lot. Because if Melvin has a love interest IN the house, he won't be needing his share of Internet time!

Home Crowded Home

Dear Diary,

Okay, two surprises in one week might just be more than my heart can handle!

If you had asked me, what's the most unlikely thing a mother and father could possibly bring up at the supper table, I still wouldn't have guessed what popped out tonight.

"We're going to have a baby. I'm four months pregnant," Mama said.

What followed was the quietest moment in the history of dinners at the Cutright family's table, and we were all there to witness it—Katrina, James, Melvin, Philip, Bobby, and me. Shell-shocked.

One of us should have said, "This is great, Mama," or "I can't wait until there's a baby in the house again, you guys," but instead Bobby asked, "Aren't you too old?" (Okay, it probably wasn't the most diplomatic thing to say, but he did break the ice.)

"I'm only thirty-eight," Mama said matter-of-factly, not even taken aback by Bobby's rudeness, "and the doctor says everything should be fine. I'm in good health, thanks to never having a minute's rest from picking up after you kids, and I don't smoke or drink."

Daddy didn't say or do anything. He just sat there with a great big goofy grin spreading from ear to ear. Daddy loves babies, no matter whose they are. He coos and goo-goos until we're all about ready to go crazy, and he blows monkey bubbles on their bellies until both he and the baby are laughing to the point of peeing on themselves.

Then it hit me, the magnitude of the whole situation. "I'm not changing diapers," I said, more to myself than to anyone else, and everyone broke into laughter.

"We'll see about that," Daddy said, "and anyway that's months from now. At the moment, I just want everyone to help your mother out around the house and pick up your own things. You're going to have to pitch in more. Your mother's not your personal slave."

The baby wasn't even here yet, and already it was making my life harder.

The boys continued to shovel in food like they wanted to get their share swallowed before the baby came and gobbled the hamburgers and macaroni and cheese right off their plates. Katrina just sat looking miserable but resigned, like she had already known and had had some time to brace herself. Mama had probably confided in her earlier, since she is the oldest. This made steam come out of my ears. I hope the baby is a sister, so we can keep secrets and never tell Mama or Katrina anything.

Then the scariest thought of all crossed my mind: It could be another brother—like Bobby, Melvin, James, or Philip! I was so close to hyperventilating that I promised myself to do a considerable amount of little-sister praying every night before I fall asleep, and every morning before I get up, and during class if I can sneak time until my baby SISTER arrives safely.

P.S. If the baby chews on you, Diary, or dares slobber on your expensive cover, I might just have to sell her to a traveling carnival.

P.P.S. Do you think Mama was trying to butter me up for the BIG news with the Internet present? If so, IT SURE HELPED!

Homeroom

Dear Diary,

When you are down and worried and traumatized, aren't friends supposed to provide comfort? Understanding? Support? Ha. Guess again.

"That's downright disgusting," said Sally, twisting up her face as if I had just told her the gruesome details of a fifty-car pileup.

"Yeah, it's perverted," said Missy. "Just think. Your parents still . . . you know. . . . I'm really sorry, Venola Mae," she said, and patted me on the back of the hand like she was offering her condolences for a dear departed loved one.

"Oh no, what if your mama starts nursing the baby in public places? I'll just die!" cried Sally.

Of all the things that ran through my head after I went to bed last night, I'd never once considered how traumatic, embarrassing, and discomforting this whole pregnancy thing was going to be for my friends.

I thought about not wanting to give up my place in the family, about not being the baby anymore, and I wondered if twelve years was long enough to be the family's baby. I kind of like being the youngest, and I'll have to admit that it helps me get my way more than occasionally when Bobby is hogging the TV, or punching me on the arm, or calling me names. "Why don't you act your age, and quit picking on your little sister?" Mama says, and I just stick my tongue out at Bobby behind her back and watch him fume. Now I'll probably be the one being told to act my age. Ugh.

I had thought about the piles of stinking diapers, and the smelly baby formulas, and all the puking and spitting up, and the oozing of slimy green and orange baby food out of her nose and mouth, and the nonstop crying jags, and the running for bottles and clean diapers and washcloths and clean baby sleepers, but never once had I thought about how embarrassed my friends would be. I guess I just always figured my parents . . . well . . . you know. . . . They still hold hands in public, and Dad still swats Mama playfully on the rear as she passes by. She runs her fingers through his hair and kisses his forehead as she hands him a cup of coffee in the morning or while they're watching TV in the evening. And with all my brothers and sisters, you just kind of figure, that's how we all got here.

Sally's an only child, and her dad left town with his secretary three years ago, and her mother openly hates all men. So I understand Sally's aversion to the whole thing, but Missy's dad still lives at home. Then again, everyone in town is always talking about Missy's mom and dad. They say how Missy's parents are the only people in town who have ever been to a marriage counselor, maybe because they arc the only ones who can afford it, and even after all that expensive counseling, they still can't stand each other and are only staying together until the children are old enough to leave home, so I guess that's why she is so weirded out by parents like mine.

7:15 P.M., Home Bored Home

Dear Diary,

My brother James is bringing the computer home tonight after he gets off work at Wal-Mart. He has promised to hook it up if he is not too tired.

I heard Mama giving him buying instructions (and a blank check) this morning. I think James was getting fed up with her advice.

"Mama, I work with money all day," he said.

"Well, if you lose the check, anyone can fill in the numbers and walk away with a brand-new car."

James started laughing. "We don't sell cars at Wal-Mart, and you've already filled in that it's to Wal-Mart for a computer, but would you feel better if you pinned it to my shirt like you did when I was in kindergarten?"

I can't be certain, but I think I saw her check her pocket for a safety pin before James made it out the door.

So until tonight, I am stuck here with not a thing

to do. I've even finished my weekend homework so that nothing can get in the way of my computer time later tonight!

P.S. I WILL ABSOLUTELY kill James if he loses that check.

9:45 P.M.

Dear Diary,

I have just spent the last two and a half hours poring through Mama's <u>Bevy of Baby Names</u> book that the doctor gave her. I found out that "Nathan" means "a gift" and <u>that</u> he <u>definitely</u> is, a drop-dead gorgeous gift that was delivered right to the door of my classroom.

At first I was looking for "Venola," but of course, my name was not listed. It never is. So instead I looked for "Sammy," which is a shortened version for "Samuel." The baby book said: "Biblical, a famous prophet and judge." So I figured this book was about as far-fetched and accurate as MASH at predicting people's destinies. If it had said "annoying" or "good with numbers" or maybe even "circus clown," I would have been a firm believer, but "famous prophet"? Sammy? Yeah, right.

I was almost ready to give up, but I decided to look for "Sally," which turned out to be a form of "Sarah," meaning "princess." Figures! That might explain why she's always trying to order me around. And Missy is a form of "Melissa," which means "honeybee." This makes ABSOLUTE perfect sense because she can be sweet once in a while, but you always have to be watching for that darned stinger to zap you.

I can never find my name anywhere, especially on any of those pre-personalized things that they have at Wal-Mart, like pencils, stationery, and note-books. Missy has a personalized license plate for her bicycle that is surrounded with pastel hearts and flowers, and she and Sally both have leather key chains with their names burned in fancy letters.

I've always wanted something with my name on it like that, so at the winter carnival a few months ago, I gave a guy twenty dollars to airbrush my name on a T-shirt with a caricature of me and a gray cat that looks like my cat Tiger Lily. I told the guy plain enough "Venola," and spelled it for him twice, but when he handed it to me, he had spelled it "Vanola."

"Sir, this isn't right. I said 'Venola.' V-e̲-n-o-l-a."
But he wasn't even listening and had gone to work on a picture of a dirt mover shirt for a little boy named Brad.

The picture of me and Tiger Lily was funny, but who wants a T-shirt that looks like you don't even know how to spell your own name? So I said, "Excuse me, this just isn't right."

He had the nerve to give me a dirty look. Well this just burned me up. He was all smiles and kind words when he wanted my money, so I said, "Hey, mister, are you going to fix this or not?"

"It's close enough. No one will notice, kid," and he went back to working on Brad's bulldozer. Then he dismissed me as cold as ice with a wave of the back of his hand. I guess he had his twenty dollars and didn't really care about customer satisfaction.

But he didn't know who he was dealing with. I marched over to the president of the carnival association, who just happens to be Sammy Potter's mom, and she came over and asked him to fix it somehow for me.

"Can't you turn the 'A' into an 'E'?" she asked politely.

I figured he would give her a dirty look too, but instead he grabbed the shirt, sprayed some white paint over the "a" and slapped an "e" in its place and tossed it back.

"That's ever so much better," she said. "Thanks a million, Mr. Hoffstettler," and off she took through the crowd. She didn't even look at how the "e" was running and smearing with the "a" which was bleeding through and just looked stupid. I bet Mrs. Potter would have cared a little more if it were her T-shirt, and I bet Mr. Hoffstettler would have taken his time and done it right if it were for an adult. Sometimes kids get bum deals from grown-ups . . . like being named "Venola."

I wish my mom had put a little more thought into how names have meanings and might affect a kid's whole life and development, instead of just naming me after dead relatives. I think I'm going to shorten it to Vennie, which the book says is related to "Vincent" and stands for "conquering." That would be something I could live with. The other one in the book that was a little close was "Venus," which would also have been okay by me because it means "goddess of beauty." Then maybe Nathan would notice that I'm more than someone for the teachers to yell at.

I decided to make Mama a list of possible names for my baby sister, so that her life is not traumatized like mine.

First, I looked up Mama and Daddy's choices so far, to try to sense a method to their madness.

Katrina: short for Katherine, "pure"
The twins, James Ronald and Philip Donald:
    named after two of the Twelve Apostles
Melvin: "friend" (my brother?)
Bobby: "bright fame" (I don't think so, unless it
    is infamy.)
Venola: does not exist on paper or in baby books.
    Does this mean I'm going to be invisible all
    my life, amount to nothing?

Then I looked through all the girl names in the baby book. Most of the names had to do with beauty and flowers and used words like "fancy, glittering, beloved, pure, sweetness." A lot had to do with being little or feminine, like "tiny bird" and "little rabbit" or "little darling" or "little one." "Caroline" and "Charlotte" both mean "little and womanly." Does that mean tall girls like me have to be "manly"?

If I have my say, my little sister will be named something a little tougher, so that she will be able to take care of herself in a bind.

Alcina—strong willed, a sorceress who rules over
    a magical land
Alyssa—logical, rational
Bernadine—brave as a bear
Bernice—she who brings victory
Billie—strong willed
Brina—protector
Bridget—power
Brunhilda—armored woman warrior
Calypso—concealer
Casey—brave, watchful
Chanda—great goddess
Colette—people of victory
Dallas—wise

Well, this is a starter kit for Mama and Daddy. Maybe they will pick one of these, and I won't have to read the whole book. My eyes are tired!

I'M NOT EVEN GOING TO LOOK FOR A BABY BROTHER'S NAME. IF IT'S A BOY, MAYBE MAMA CAN TRADE WITH SOMEONE AT THE HOSPITAL FOR A GIRL, OR SEND IT BACK TO BE EXCHANGED. Ha. Ha. Please, God, give me a sister to even the odds a little!

P.S. James is FINALLY here with the computer! Hurray.

```
Dear Sally,
  This is a test. Write me when (IF) you
get this!
Venola Mae Cutright

P.S. I am SO excited!
```

Dear Sally,

   Hurray! I can't believe how fast you can get my words on your computer. It's almost like being psychics or spies or something. Not much has happened since we talked on the phone an hour ago, except I learned that your name means "princess" and mine doesn't even exist. Bummer.

Later,

Venola

**From:** "Venola"<cutright1@mtnbelle.net>
**To:** "Sally"<scathell@mtnbelle.net>
**Subject: Bedtime, Anyone?**
**Date:** Sunday, March 12; Time: 23:35

Dear S.,
    This is great! Now we can do this all
the time—except for now. Mama says it
is time for bed.
Good night,
Love,
Ven

P.S. Thanks for saying you like my name.

Homeroom

Dear Diary,

I am so sleepy, and my eyes are burning. I guess staring at the baby book, staying awake while James hooked up the Internet, AND writing to Sally wore me out. I've got to learn to type faster than with two fingers.

Sally is tired too. She seemed kind of cranky on the bus this morning.

I had a chance to show off Gwen to her. "There she is!" I said, pointing through the steamy bus window. Gwen was standing in front of the post office, holding hands with Melvin.

Instead of riding our bus like he's supposed to, Melvin now walks all the way to town each morning so he can wait with Gwen and sit next to her on the way to the high school. He's usually so lazy he won't even walk the half mile to the grocery store for Mama unless his car is broken down. But for Gwen, he'll get up a half hour earlier and walk almost TWO miles. It must be TRUE LOVE.

"If I could look like any woman on the face of this earth, I'd choose Gwen," I said.

"Too pale," said Sally, shaking her head and wrinkling her nose, dismissing Gwen as if she were one of Cinderella's ugly stepsisters. "I would rather be tan like the girls on <u>Baywatch</u>. I already have the blond hair like Pamela Anderson Lee. Too bad we don't have a beach in West Virginia where I could lay out and get some sun."

"You wouldn't really want to look like that Barbie doll, would you? You are much prettier," I said.

"Are you kidding? I'd give anything to look like a Barbie doll. Guys like Barbie dolls."

"I heard that to have the proportions of a Barbie in real life, a woman would have to have some ribs removed to be that skinny."

"You are gross, Venola Mae," said Sally, clutching her ribs like they might fall off.

Sally thinks the only thing that is keeping her from being Pamela Anderson Lee's double is that Belington doesn't have sunny beaches like California. Never mind that Sally's chest is about ten times smaller and that she burns lobster red instead of tans. I used to be kind of jealous of Sally's being a cheerleader and her good looks, even though I'd never admit it to her, but lately she's been suffering from more than occasional acne and has become a little on the chubby side. I think it might be harder to have once had good looks and to be on the verge of losing them, than never to have had them, like me. Maybe that's why Sally's been moodier than usual lately.

I don't know if it was because Sally had been bossing me around all week or just because Gwen has been really nice to me, but I felt it was my duty to take up for Gwen's looks. "I think Gwendolyn has what's called 'classic beauty,' and she doesn't have to worry about monthly dye jobs, lip injections, and tanning to make her radiant and glamorous," I said. "She knows how to dress too. Bracelets galore and a ring on every finger."

"Gee, Venola Mae, are you sure you're in love with Gwendolyn's brother? Sounds like you have a crush on Gwendolyn instead." She pulled out a mirror and started looking at her not-so-blond roots.

Neither of us are really morning people, especially after yesterday's late-night E-mail session, and I knew Sally was just being silly about me having a crush on Gwen. So in order to keep from not speaking to each other the rest of the day, or maybe even the entire week, like has happened before, I didn't acknowledge her wisecrack with a comeback, although I did snort a little.

Sure, I like Gwen. She's been at my house more lately than Katrina, Philip, and James put together. My two oldest brothers and sister are either at work, or out on dates, but Gwen comes home with Melvin to our house almost every afternoon because they are serious about studying and getting into the same medical school somewhere.

Gwen is supernice, and unlike a lot of sixteen-year-old girls, she even asks me (a twelve-year-old!) what I think about things, like makeup and hair and clothes, just like I'm a real person.

She doesn't even care if I stay in the room while she and Melvin study. And I'm doing my best to be on my good behavior and not to annoy them like I usually do when one of my brothers brings someone over. I heard her tell Melvin it helps keep his mind on schoolwork when I'm around. I'm pretty sure he wants to hire a hit man to come and vaporize me, but when I told Gwen this, she laughed and said she will protect me to the best of her ability.

When they talk about their future together, and college and medical school, they get all dreamy-looking and stare into each other's eyes big time. They are only sixteen and juniors in high school, but I bet they get married someday. I'll probably get to be maid of honor, unless Melvin wins the lottery and can afford a good hit man before then.

I wonder if Nathan wants to go to medical school. We've never had a real conversation other than when I said "thank you" that time when I dropped my pencil and he grunted a kind of "you're welcome."

Sally must have known my mind was somewhere

else other than on our stimulating conversation about the merits of looking like a <u>Baywatch</u> girl because she poked me in the ribs, a little harder than what I would consider necessary.

"Where were you? Dreaming about Nathan or his lovely sister Gwendolyn?" she asked, with a don't-be-mad-at-me devilish grin.

"Very funny. Too bad your future husband Jonathan Cruthers is going out with Rebecca Watkins. Kind of gets in the way of your own wedding plans and the mansion with the dozen kids and minivan, doesn't it?"

Sally just laughed. That MASH game and her impending betrothal to the older man were forgotten days ago, and she was obsessed with winning her ex-boyfriend, A.J., back from Lynette Cross again. But unlike Sally's fickle nature, my own attraction for and fascination with Nathan was growing hourly.

Lunch

Dear Diary,

You are lucky to be flat pieces of paper minding your own business inside my backpack instead of having to deal with nosy-body humans.

Sally decided to take it upon herself to be match-maker for me today. There we were (Sally, Missy, and me) sitting in the gym after lunch, listening to some CDs, talking about bathing suits, eating junk food, and watching the guys play basketball when Sally got the bright idea that my relationship with Nathan wasn't moving fast enough to suit her.

"It's been a whole week, Venola, and you are no closer to going out with him now than you were that first day when he floated over from Gallipolis."

"So, I'm in no hurry," I said, even though deep down I am because I have never had a boyfriend before, and all of my other girlfriends have. But for some reason I couldn't let on to Sally and Missy that I cared, so I kept thumbing through Missy's <u>Selena's Specialties</u> catalog to give the impression I didn't give a hoot one way or another whether Nathan wanted to be my boyfriend or not. "Mama and Daddy probably wouldn't let me go OUT out anyway," I finally said.

"That's not the point. You could watch TV over the phone with him, or listen to the radio and try to get through the request line to dedicate songs to each other, or a whole gang of us could go to the movies together some Saturday night. I'm not saying he has to rent a limousine and take just you out for dinner and dancing. Chill, girl." Sally looked around the gymnasium with purpose. "I'm going to send Sammy over to see if Nathan likes you at all," she said, and waved for Sammy to come to us.

Luckily, Sammy was too involved in entertaining two eighth-grade majorettes with his latest attempt at card tricks to even acknowledge Sally's beckoning, although you'd think he surely couldn't miss her high-pitched screeching of his name that went along with the wave. "Sammy! Sammy Potter! YOU-hoo!"

I could feel my face turning bloodred. "Sally, if you dare mention me or Nathan to Sammy, you are no longer my best friend," I threatened. I didn't really mean it though, and I hoped she'd sneak around behind my back and find out the verdict for me. But I'd only want to know if it were good news. If he were repulsed by me, I think it would be easier to go on living if Sally kept the truth from me. Do you suppose he IS repulsed by me?

But my window of opportunity for Sally to care

enough to send a messenger closed, at least for the moment. She has never listened to me before when it came to my asking her not to meddle. Why now? She just shrugged her shoulders, like it was my loss, screamed "never mind" to Sammy, who had finally started sauntering up the bleachers toward us, and then she changed the subject.

"Pass the potato chips," I said as I handed Sally the Doritos, while I tried to think of a way to hint that I wouldn't really get TOO angry if she sent a messenger to find out you know what from Nathan.

Study Hall

Dear Diary,

Are boys born troublemakers?

Thanks to Sammy, we can no longer bring Selena's Specialties or any catalogs with underwear and bathing suits in them to school, even to look at in our own free time during recess.

Too bad for us that Sammy decided to join us even though Sally called, "Never mind." I guess the eighth-grade majorettes had grown tired of his card tricks and shooed him away, so he decided to settle for us three mere seventh graders.

"What are you all so absorbed in?" he asked, and pushed his way into our private little circle, making room for his rear right between Missy and me by poking us with his bony little elbows.

"Wow! Where did you find that?" he asked and tried to turn the page while the rest of us were still looking.

"Back off, birdbrain!" Missy yelled. "This is my catalog from home, and I don't want your greasy grubby fingerprints all over it! This conversation is between A," she said, pointing to herself, "and B," she said, pointing to me and Sally, "so C your way out of it!"

Well, maybe he didn't like her tone, or maybe he would have done it anyway, but Sammy grabbed the catalog and took off running down the bleachers and across the gym floor. Missy and Sally and I followed screaming, but he was out the door and into the lunchroom to show his buddies before we had a fair chance to catch up.

When we caught up and pleaded our case to Mr. Fenstermacher, who was on lunch duty, he called Sammy over and asked to hear both sides of the story. Then he confiscated the catalog and sent us back to the gymnasium with a lecture ending, "Never bring smut like this to school again." Sammy didn't even get a day's detention!

**From:** "Venola"<cutright1@mtnbelle.net>
**To:** <mknox@mtnbelle.net>
**Subject: Guess Who?**
**Date:** Monday, March 13; Time: 17:36

Dear Mrs. Knox,

 My brothers and I were goofing around on the Internet, and we found your name, address, phone number, AND E-mail address! Our new computer is fantastic! (I just wish the boys would give me more time on it. What hogs!)

 But the good news is now I can write to you and the other teachers any time I have questions about homework or something! Or even if I'm just bored and need someone to talk to! Isn't the Internet cool?

 Write back soon!
One of your favorite English (and home-room) students,
And your new pen pal,
Venola Mae Cutright

P.S. You aren't going to circle my mistakes and give this back like you do in class, are you?

**From:** "Venola"<cutright1@mtnbelle.net>
**To:** "Sally"<scathell@mtnbelle.net>
**Subject: GIRLS AGAINST CENSORSHIP AND
  CATALOG THIEVES**
**Date:** Monday, March 13; Time:17:42


Dear S.,
   Too bad about Missy's lingerie catalog.
She can't even complain to her mom
because Mrs. Fowler FORBADE her to take
it to school in the first place. Mothers
can be so uptight!
   That mean old Mr. Fenstermacher. Do
you think it's true what they say—that
he wears a toupee?

Monday, March 13

5:50 P.M., Home Prison Home


Dear Diary,

There is no privacy in this house! Mama came up behind me while I was writing to Sally on the computer, and she has threatened to have the "WHOLE THING" taken out if I write such "negative gossip" again.

Bummer.

**From:** "Venola"<cutright1@mtnbelle.net>
**To:** "Sally"<scathell@mtnbelle.net>
**Subject: TOP SECRET**
**Date:** Monday, March 13; Time: 17:55

```
Dear Sally,
   I agree that we need a secret code
system, but what? Keep thinking.
Me
```

Homeroom

Dear Diary,

I asked Mrs. Knox if she received my E-mail, but she said her computer is broken, and she doesn't know if she is ever going to have it fixed. She said I should just talk to her in class if I have questions about assignments, and that she never assigns anything for homework that is so important that it can't wait until morning if I don't understand it.

I asked Mrs. Proudfoot, Mr. Bookout, and the rest of my teachers for their E-mail addresses, but they all said they are having problems with their Internet connections too.

Dear Diary,

Sally and I are devising our own system. Well, some of it we picked up from other kids at school.

From now on, if an adult comes into the room while we are typing, we are going to stop writing our juicy stuff, type M911 (Mama alert) or D911 (Dad alert) or B911 (brother alert), and send the message midsentence.

How many of these codes should we come up with? Do we need an alert for grandparents, aunts, uncles, friends, preachers, neighbors, the Avon lady??? Ahhhh. This could get confusing if we have to stop and think about our relationship to the invader! For my Parkersburg cousins, would I type "C" for cousin or "F" for friends, or maybe "CF" because they are both!!! Maybe we should just do 911 for all those not in the immediate family.

P.S. I wonder how it will be once the baby gets here. Will Mama have less time to read my E-mails (hurray!), or will I have less computer time because of extra BABY chores? Ugh.

54

Home Too Weird Home

Dear Diary,

Mama says Nathan's parents are joining our church Sunday, AND that she has invited them for lunch the Sunday after next. This can't be happening. That only gives me a little over a week to clean my room AND to plan what I'm going to wear. NO ONE could clean my room in a month, let alone ELEVEN days. What was Mama thinking? Will Nathan think that I'm a complete slob? Or that I am a baby because I still have stuffed animals and dolls in my room? Should I hide them? Box them up for the baby to chew on?

I have one animal that is OFF LIMITS to the little drooler. I'm not ready to part with my Samoyed that I won at last year's fair. I spent twenty-three dollars tossing rings over pop bottles to get that dog because it is like the dogs from one of my all-time favorite books, Stone Fox. I could probably have bought the thing cheaper in a store, but I had never seen a Samoyed stuffed animal before. It looks real and is SO soft. I like to bury my fingers in its fur as I drift off to sleep. Don't tell.

I can pick up all my clothes and stuff, and pile them in the closet. That's no big deal, as long as no one touches the closet door, that is.

If I beg Sally, will she help me rearrange my furniture? She has really good taste when it comes to interior decorating and changes hers all the time. My furniture has always been in the same spots. I never thought it mattered because my room is so small. I never realized how ugly the whole place is before. I wonder if Mama would let me paint my room. If so, maybe I should find out what color Nathan likes best. Would blue be more sophisticated than this stupid mint green? Should I buy some posters of rock groups? I wonder which groups are his favorites?

Help!!!!!!!

Top Secret Vital Statistics of Nathan Racin

Can be seen at the following locations:

Locker at 8:25–8:35, 11:55–12:00, and 2:35–2:40.

Water fountain—between every period. Does he do it to take up time so he won't have to talk to anyone, or does he have a problem with his sugar like Grandma? She drinks a lot too.

Bathroom—varies, but usually between third and fourth period, and sixth and seventh. (Maybe someone should clue him in about the connection between this and his never-ending trips to the water fountain!)

Lunch table—Fifth from the right, next to Sammy Potter and Joe Westerman. Eats hot lunch except on fish stick day, and usually trades his desserts to someone at his table for extra entrees, especially on chili day. He always trades his brownie to Tommy Flint for half a peanut butter sandwich.

Favorite color: Always wears blue or black T-shirts.

Favorite sports: Likes them all, but exceptionally good at basketball during lunch hour. Sweats more than average. Ugh. Should bring second shirt from home for changing before afternoon classes. PU.

Most serious competition: Not sure. Probably Missy. I've seen her talking to him five times at his locker. All the girls flirt with him and giggle at anything he says, even Sally. Growl! But I don't think Sally would go after him, would she? After all, she was just trying to fix us up the other day, wasn't she???? Should I give up? Do I have a chance with him?

Miscellaneous Nathan Facts Gathered from Other Sources:

From Gwen: Good at yard darts and Nintendo, loves <u>Star Trek</u> and alien movies, has read every <u>Animorph</u> book written, and collects them in hardback editions.

From Sammy: Does not like any girl in particular, never cheats at sports, and not really interested in card tricks.

Venola Mae Racin

Mrs. Nathan Racin

Mrs. Nathan Racin III

Venola Mae Cutright Racin

Venola M. Cutright Racin

Venola Racin

Mr. and Mrs. Nathan Racin

Venola Mae Racin

Mrs. Racin

Venola and Nathan

Nathan and Venola Racin

Mrs. Venola M. Racin

Venola Cutright Racin

Mr. & Mrs. Nathan Racin III

V. M. R.

Home Sneaky Home

Dear Diary,

I've always heard if you want something done right, you have to do it yourself, so I figured I might as well take the initiative in my relationship with Nathan. Detective work is easy for someone as crafty as I am. The key is to act as if the information you are searching for is no big deal, and then people give it up willingly without even having a clue.

"Hey, Gwen, I'm making a list of baby names for Mama, and was just wondering what's your middle name?" I asked this afternoon.

Gwen, as always, was sitting next to Melvin with her nose in a book. "Mariah," she said without even looking up.

"Ooo, that has a nice ring to it, 'Gwendolyn Mariah Racin.' Your mother must have a knack for names. What did she pick for your brother?"—I never use his real name with Gwen, because I don't want to appear overly interested. Gwen is very intuitive and likely to catch on. Plus I'm afraid I might start to blush if I say "Nathan."

"Nothing too original. It's Randall," she said. "He

hates it and is always saying he wishes he had something tougher like 'Chip' or 'Buzz.' He's named after our grandfather." She smiled and went back to reading.

"Does your brother like it here? Or does he miss his old friends from where you used to live? Some of the girls were taking bets whether he had a girlfriend there because he doesn't seem to pay any attention to them," I hinted. Maybe she'd say something about an old Gallipolis girlfriend, or that she thought he liked me or something.

No such luck today. Gwen's mind was definitely on studying for her test. "I'm not sure," she said. "We don't talk that much. You know how brothers and sisters are sometimes." She motioned toward Melvin and winked at me.

Boy, did I. Melvin was giving me the "get lost" look at that very moment, but that was fine with me because I was leaving anyway. I had all the information I needed for now, and I'd found it less than two minutes after Sally had told me it was necessary to my future happiness with Nathan. Plus I had the bonus knowledge that as far as Gwen knew, Nathan wasn't pining away for some Gallipolis babe that he had been forced to leave behind.

So I went back to my room to call Sally. (Some things are just too complicated for explaining over E-mail.) She had been really upset because I didn't know Nathan's middle name. "You've got to find out if you want it to be accurate, Venola Mae! Love/Marriage/Hate/Divorce won't work with just first and last names." According to Sally, to find out if Nathan and I are compatible, she has to know the exact number of letters in the FULL name, and you can't cheat and just use first, partial, or nicknames.

"Randall," I said into the receiver when Sally said "Hello?" Now it was time for the true test, according to Dr. Sally Cathell, Love Counselor at Large.

Nathan Randall Racin
Venola Mae Cutright

"Love, marriage, hate, divorce, love, marriage, hate, divorce," she chanted as she carefully counted each letter in both of our names until she came to the last letter in my name. "HATE! Oh no. You're going to end up hating Nathan or he's going to end up hating you, if the two of you make the mistake of marrying, Venola. You won't get divorced, but according to this test, you're going to rue the day you ever say 'I do' to the likes of Nathan Randall Racin. Maybe you won't be able to stand his bad breath or the way he burps real loud after every meal or chews popcorn with his mouth open at the movies and drowns out the funny lines, but you'll probably stay with him for the kids and be miserable until one of the two of you finally takes pity on the other and dies."

"I wonder if this is why Missy's parents don't get along. Do you think their marriage counselor thought to do the Love/Marriage/Hate/Divorce test on their names?" I asked, trying to get Sally to lighten up and move off of my doomed future marriage to Nathan and on to someone else's woes.

Then it came to me. "Sally, stop! It's going to be okay. I forgot to tell you, Nathan's name is really Nathan Randall Racin III. So that means you have to add Divorce/Love/Marriage!"

Sally started making a funny clicking sound with her tongue. "Sorry, Venola, but I think numbers just count as one, which ends you in divorce, but on the bright side you won't have to stay around listening to him burp and crunch his popcorn for the rest of your life, or the rest of his, whichever ends first." Sometimes I don't think Sally actually wants me to be happy.

Until Sally checks around with her experts and the verdict comes back, I'm going by my way of counting. Wouldn't you?

S.,
  I don't ever want to go back. I know I
was stupid, but how could YOU laugh with
her? Do you like Missy better?
Depressed,
Me

**From:** "Venola"<cutright1@mtnbelle.net>
**To:** 'fessup@youngandstylish.com
**Subject: EMERGENCY ADVICE REQUESTED**
**Date:** Friday, March 17; Time: 16:45

Dear Young and Stylish Magazine Editor,
   I read your magazine every month
(since my mother got it for me for my
birthday last October). I especially like
your 'Fess Up column where everyone
writes in with their most humiliating
experiences, and although I'm a poster
child for embarrassing moments, I've
never had anything to compete with your
readers until now.
   This morning I was walking to gym
class, and it's a long way to the girls'
locker room once you enter the gym.
Anyway, it was a girls' only gym class
day, all the boys were in health class,
and I thought I was all alone in the
gym. I don't know what possessed me.
Maybe it was that fashion show on CNN
the other night. Well, I decided to walk
like a runway fashion model, and I
walked all the way across the gym floor
while REALLY swinging my hips from side
to side, in what I thought would be a
sexy walk. You've probably guessed it —I
WASN'T ALONE! A girl (named Missy) who I
don't like that much anyway and my (as
of today) ex-best friend, Sally, were

behind me to see the whole performance, and they came into the locker room laughing their heads off, imitating my jiggly walk.

Then Missy told the rest of the girls, so when everyone was dressed for gym, EVERYBODY went swinging into the gym, chanting "Boom-da-dee-boom, da-dee-boom. . . ." I want to die. Should I switch schools now, or will this die down?

If you decide to publish this, I'd rather you not use my name in your magazine. Help.

Dear S.,

You really thought I knew you and Missy were there, and I was doing it to be funny? No way!

And I don't believe you have EVER done anything as embarrassing. Give one example.

Venola

Okay, okay. I only asked for one. Thanks for making me laugh (so hard I spit out water on the keyboard). I hadn't thought about how you threw up on Missy's desk in fourth grade in a long time.

Will you really make the gagging sound as you go by her desk on Monday? You'd do this for me? Which class? Our secret, right?

Feeling better,
Me (aka Boom-da-dee-boom)

**From:** "Venola"<cutright1@mtnbelle.net>
**To:** 'fessup@youngandstylish.com
**Subject: NEVER MIND!**
**Date:** Friday, March 17; Time: 17:11


Dear Young and Stylish Magazine Editor,
  Regarding my E-mail to you of a few
hours ago, NEVER MIND! (If you still want
to use it in your column, that would
be cool.)
Sincerely,
Boom-da-dee-boom

Dear Diary,

Only one week until Nathan comes to my house. Everything must be PERFECT. Mama says we are going to grill outside if the weather is pretty. PLEASE don't let it rain because Mama's hamburgers bubbling in a greasy old skillet do not compare to those sizzling on the grill. Yummm.

I just called the weather station, but they only give a three-day forecast. I'll have to keep checking.

S.,

Do you think I should wear my green T-shirt when Nathan comes over? I think it looks the best on me (or as good as anything can). Ugh. I wish I looked like anyone but me.

Then again, maybe I should wear blue or black because those seem to be Nathan's favorite colors. Please advise.

Too much to think about and too little time left until the big event.

Getting Anxious,

V.

Dear Diary,

Just think, next week HE will be here.

Room is looking SOME better, but it is really hard
to part with things that I have been collecting for
twelve years. I pick up a story that I wrote in fifth
or sixth grade and start reading it, and think about
how I could make it better now, or how stupid the
whole idea is, and then I spend time on that instead
of organizing my stacks of papers. Then hours pass
and all I've done is daydream or start reading one
of my favorite books that I pull out from under my
bed, amid piles of dirty socks and various other
unmentionables.

ALL my papers and books and journals and notes
are important. I don't know what I'll need when
I'm a famous freelance writer or journalist, actress,
or shark trainer. Maybe I'll use these things in my
memoirs.

Maybe I should just buy some huge Rubbermaid
containers and toss all my papers in like a time
capsule, not to be opened until I'm old and incredibly
rich and famous.

Dear S.,
   I don't know what to think. That really
freaked me out today. Do you think they
have done it before? I've heard Karla
and Missy bragging about shoplifting a
couple of times, but I thought they were
just talking big in front of the older
girls.
   The thing is, I was RIGHT THERE, and I
didn't see them do it. What if they had
gotten caught? We would have been in
trouble too!
Ven

Dear Diary,

I've got to tell someone this or bust, so you are elected. Today Missy, Karla, Sally, and I got off the bus in town, and went to the grocery store for some junk food, and then we went into the drugstore because Missy said she needed to get "a couple of things," so we were all looking at makeup, and saying goofy stuff like, "This would look FABULOUS on you, dawling!" and we'd hold up a really nasty shade of blue eye shadow or avocado green lipstick. Then the clerk came over and asked us to quiet down or leave, so we all left.

Well, when we got outside, Missy and Karla started showing us what they had taken. About six different flavors of lip gloss. And I thought Missy had marched out without buying her things because the clerk made her mad!!! How naive can I get? What if they had gotten caught? I'm never ever going in a store with them again. Why would they do this? Their families have lots more money than mine, and even I can afford my own lip gloss!

P.S. Okay, here's the worst part. They gave Sally and me each a lip gloss. I told Missy no, but she just said she had plenty, and to stick it in my purse. Sally did, so I did too. I feel like that tube of lip gloss weighs 500 pounds.

P.P.S. I tasted it. Yuck, watermelon.

P.P.P.S. It wouldn't matter anyway. I don't think I could wear it even if it were something good like green apple or cinnamon.

P.P.P.P.S. What should I do with it?

S.,
  No, tell them I won't tell. But I'm
not going in the drugstore (or any
stores) with them again. You shouldn't
either.
Ven

P.S. I don't care if they do think I'm
a big baby.

**From:** "Venola"<cutright1@mtnbelle.net>
**To:** 'fessup@youngandstylish.com
**Subject: Shoplifting Friends**
**Date:** Monday, March 20; Time: 20:22

Dear Young and Stylish Magazine Editor,
   I just found out that these two girls
I know shoplift all the time. I'm NEVER
going in a store with them again! Okay,
here's my question: If they gave me some
stolen lip gloss, what should I do?
   Please don't use my name in your
column. Thank you.
Anonymous

P.S. If I don't tell on them, am I
guilty too?

Home No Privacy Home

Dear Diary,

I think Mama must have found my vital statistics about Nathan or the three pages of Mrs. Nathan Racin that I wrote and stuck under my pillow because she has decided it is time for "the talk." When she came in my room with that serious look, I thought the drugstore had called, or that she somehow knew that I'd stuffed stolen watermelon lip gloss into the bottom of my sock drawer.

But all she wanted to do was talk about "the birds and the bees."

I told her that I wasn't interested in boys "like that yet," and that the health teacher had already talked to us about the facts of life way back in fifth grade. (It was a big deal. All of us girls got to go to the cafeteria with Nurse Betty, and she showed us a film and let us ask lots and lots of questions. The gym teacher took all the boys to the gym and showed them a film and then asked if anyone had questions, but no one did, so they got to play several games of dodgeball until all of us girls were finished talking to Nurse Betty.)

Mama wasn't ready to drop the subject yet.

"Well, sometimes a mother can explain things better," and she proceeded with her speech about "the birds and the bees."

I tried to tell her I was too young to even consider such stuff, but she went on to tell me about her stepgrandmother, who was married and pregnant at thirteen. It turns out that when Mama's real grandmother died bearing her sixth child, my great-grandpa Hanson chose to remarry right away, probably because he wasn't excited about dealing with six children alone, especially a newborn. So his best friend obliged by handing over his oldest daughter, Juanita, which Mama said "meant one less mouth to feed."

I couldn't imagine someone my age being a stepmother OR a mother. "She was thirteen and pregnant, AND had six stepchildren to take care of? I'll be thirteen in six and a half months, and I don't even want to change diapers for your ONE baby!" I threw myself backward on the bed.

"Juanita wasn't given much of a choice. And the strange part had to be that she had stepchildren older than she was. Your grandfather was seventeen, and your two great-aunts would have been around fourteen and twelve. Can you imagine being the stepmother to girls your age, like your friends Missy and Sally? I guess Great-aunt Dory and Elke gave poor Juanita a pretty hard time too. Then there was an eight-year-old and a five-year-old and the baby to take care of. Makes us thankful for the life we were dealt, doesn't it?" Mama said, straightening my hair from inside my shirt collar.

"Definitely."

"Changing a diaper for a little sister or brother all of a sudden doesn't sound too bad, does it?" Mama said, hinting at my future.

"I'm not answering that," I said, but grinned, and I leaned my head over on Mama's stomach to see if the baby would kick. "She" had started saying "hello" lately.

P.S. Should I take the lip gloss money to the drugstore and leave it on the counter? I think I will.

Dear Sal,

Nathan better be worth it! I feel like
a prisoner of my own room. Even Bobby has
been stopping by my room to check on me,
and to try to get me going with his
insults. I guess he misses me picking on
him and his friends when they come over.
Tee hee.

Daddy asked Mama what I had done to
get grounded, and she said she couldn't
remember. I had to REMIND them that 1 am
not grounded, merely a free spirit who
simply is tired of living in a pigpen.
Feeling better,
V.

P.S. Don't tell Missy and Karla, but I
left two dollars beside the drugstore
cash register when no one was looking.

Dear S.,
  I am not a Goody Two-shoes. I just
want to be able to sleep with a clear
conscience.
  Thanks for helping me rearrange things!
Do you really think my room looks MUCH
bigger with my bookshelf jammed behind
my headboard? The bad thing is that I
can only get to my top row of books now!!
What am I supposed to do if I get the
urge to read one of the books from the
lower shelf when you aren't around to
help me lift it?
Bookless,
V.

Dear S.,

You would not sacrifice books forever for true love! Would you? Even <u>Young and Stylish</u> magazine? You love reading that as much as I do!

Well, even if you are right, I wish I'd moved all my favorite books to the top shelf before we rearranged the heavy furniture.

V.


P.S. Is this why some people act like airheads and stare into space when they are in love? Have they all pushed their beds up against their bookcases in the name of fashion?

P.P.S. Mama said N-O to my request to paint my room navy blue or black, even though I said I would use my own paper route money. She said that her queasy stomach couldn't handle the fumes, and that they might not be good for the baby, AND that it would make my room seem as small as a postage stamp. When I asked her if I could do it this summer when the windows could be open, she said, "We'll see," and went back to hanging up

laundry. That's usually as good as a no.
I also heard her tell Daddy when she
thought I wasn't in listening range that
she hoped this strange fascination to
paint my room a depressing color wore
off before the baby was born and she no
longer had morning sickness as an excuse.
AND even worse, she said she thought that
those dark colors might do permanent
damage to a baby's development and sleep
patterns. IS THAT BABY SUPPOSED TO SLEEP
IN MY ROOM??? Why MY room? Bobby's is
MUCH bigger. I hadn't even considered
such a thing!!!
P.P.P.S. Ask your mom if I can move in
with you!

**From:** "Venola"<cutright1@mtnbelle.net>
**To:** "Sally"<scathell@mtnbelle.net>
**Subject: Make Room for Baby?**
**Date:** Wednesday, March 22; Time: 21:25

Sally,
   Maybe I should leave the floor covered
with my things. If I pick everything up,
they might move a crib in sooner than I
want! Shouldn't babies sleep in the same
room with their parents???
Needing my own space,
Venola

Dear Diary,

I'm beginning to wonder if anyone ever goes together very long in seventh grade. This year Karla and Jason hold the record because they have gone together since November, which is almost five whole months. They've had little tiffs where they yell at each other in the hallways and storm away from each other's lockers, and won't sit together at lunch, and they come close to breaking up on a regular basis, but so far she has kept his ID bracelet the whole time, and he has her birthstone pinky ring around his neck on a chain under his shirt so all the guys can't see it and give him a hard time.

She doesn't even want him to take the necklace off in gym class or when he plays basketball at lunch. Rumor has it that Karla checks it several times a day to make sure he hasn't lost it rough-housing, and to make sure that in gym class, a death stinger ball hasn't gone and cracked her precious gemstone that was sent to her from her grandma who lives in Florida.

At least one day a week someone is taking up a pool as to whether the couple will make it through the day or stay together long enough to see their picture come out in the yearbook as "cutest couple." Right now, Sally is in second place for longest-running cutest couple, and I think she's hoping Karla and Jason break up. But I think Sally's claim to second place is debatable because she counts that she has been with A.J. for almost two and a half months this year, but it hasn't been all at once, so I'm not sure it should count. They have made it to three weeks, three different times, and one week two times, and then he goes and does something to make her mad (it doesn't take much!), and they don't talk for a few weeks. I don't think that even compares to Karla and Jason's record. But I'm not telling Sally this because I'd rather have her mad at A.J. than me. That girl can hold a grudge!

The only problem with Karla is she has to take the ID bracelet off and hide it in her purse before she gets home from school every day. Her mom almost had a coronary attack when Karla went home with Jason's bracelet the first day and was all excited because they were going out. Karla's mom says kids our age are too young to "go steady," and Karla's sure her mom would throw a fit and "go through the ceiling" if she found out that Karla still had the bracelet, so on the school bus every day like clockwork, Karla wraps it in two layers of tissues and stores it in the bottom of her change purse.

I think this is romantic, just like Romeo and Juliet, except I don't think Karla and Jason are ready to die for each other. They fight too much. (I just have one little question that I haven't mentioned to Karla. What's going to happen when her mom sees her yearbook, and Karla is part of the cutest couple??? Either the girl isn't thinking ahead, or she plans to deal with that situation when the time gets here!)

P.S. I guess even if Nathan and I started going out tomorrow, we couldn't win as cutest couple because there are only two more months of school left. Darn. I really would have liked that.

Dear Sally,

Trouble in Romance Land! Word around the kingdom is the Evil Faye claims Nathan as her own. Do I give in to this diabolic force, or try to thwart her once and for all for true love?

Venola

P.S. Is true love worth dying for? Yes or No?

Math Class, Fourth Period

Dear Diary,

What a day already! Missy told me during gym class that Faye Roads likes Nathan too, and that she is determined to make Nathan go with her no matter what. I guess no one took the time over the last couple of weeks to mention to Faye that Nathan is mine OR almost mine.

Faye Roads is the meanest and biggest girl in seventh grade. I have personally seen her beat up a boy for accidentally bumping into her in the hallway, and she's pretty much warned all of us girls since kindergarten that we're not even allowed to look at her the wrong way or we might not live to regret it. The problem is none of us know what the wrong or right way to look at her is.

So here's the dilemma. Do I hand over my chance of dating the best-looking guy in the school to this she-devil, and walk away still breathing, hopefully without any scratches, bruises, or arm slings? Or do I stand up to the bully, and go for what (or whom) I want in life?

Well, this is pretty much what the note I just passed to Sally in class asked. Unlike Sally's usually quick service, she hasn't responded to my cry for relationship advice. I guess she's either afraid of getting caught passing notes again or perplexed about the relationship issue, since it involves life or death (mine!), and that's why she's taking some extra time weighing all the options in order to make the right decision.

Oops. Mrs. Proudfoot's working her way down my row. Gotta go!

Lunch

Dear Diary,

I'm in big trouble! The note did not make it to Sally at all.

"What note?" Sally asked, when we finally met up at the salad bar.

"Ha. Ha. Very funny," I said, and reached for the spoon to the instant chocolate pudding. I stirred it to make sure there weren't any UFOs (unidentified floating objects). Last week some heinous pudding hater had caught the lunch monitor not paying attention and had mixed in pepperoni chunks and bacon bits. At first I thought it was just an accidental slip from a sloppy salad bar user, but there were just too many chunks for that. It was premeditated.

"I'm serious, Venola Mae. What note?" Sally asked, and I could tell by her tone that she wasn't messing around.

"Please say you are kidding, or I am SO dead." I dropped the spoon back into the pudding container, suddenly having lost my appetite, even for chocolate. "A note about Faye wanting Nathan, and about whether to give him up and live or to stand up for love and die?"

"Faye likes Nathan? No way!" she squealed, eyes big as saucers. "Who told you?" Now on a normal day this last comment would have made me mad because I think Sally was insinuating that she was the gatekeeper of all important information, and that I was just kept in the loop because I was her friend. But today I was too upset to take offense.

"I can't go into all that right now," I said. "We've got to locate that darned note before it gets into the wrong hands, if it's not already too late!"

"I never saw it. Who did you pass it to? Did you go Karla-Missy-Sammy-me, or did you go Plan B straight across the third row?"

"I don't know. I'm so confused now. I think I started to go Plan B, but then realized Jason was absent, and I was afraid it would get intercepted by Mrs. Proudfoot if they went stretching across his empty desk!"

"Okay, then we just have to check with Karla, Missy, and Sammy. Why didn't you watch it being passed, goofball!"

"It's not my fault!" I said. "Mrs. Proudfoot's the one who called on me to put that stupid word problem on the board, and it was out of my control."

The thought of my love life being reviewed by the whole seventh grade (especially Faye) made me want to crawl under a rock and die, which would definitely be better if I went ahead and did it before Faye read the note.

Sally has gone on a fact-finding mission and is going to try to sweet-talk the detention hall teacher into letting her speak to Sammy. I can't do anything but wait.

Study Hall

Dear Diary,
Note Update:

My future may be shorter than I thought.

"Missy and Karla SAY they both passed your note on," said Sally before study hall started. "I haven't been able to talk to Sammy yet. Even though I begged, Mr. Fenstermacher wouldn't let Sammy out of detention hall even for a minute."

"Do you think we can trust that Missy and Karla passed it on?" I asked. Missy and I had been getting along lately because she's a little upset at Karla for spending all her time with Jason. That's the way Missy does Sally and me. When she's mad at her best friend, she starts eating lunch with us and says we're her second-best friends, but I think she means Sally because they are both cheerleaders. I'm probably her next-to-last best friend, or maybe not even that high up on the list. Half the school would probably have to catch malaria and drop dead before I would be her first-best friend, which is okay by me because I just don't trust her. Now, as for Karla, I don't think she is out to get me, but then again if Missy said, "Don't pass the note," I think Karla would do whatever she said because she is pretty much Missy's robot.

Sally gave me a really weird look, like I was suddenly from a different planet. "Sure, why wouldn't you trust them? Did you hear something?" Sally trusts everyone until they cross her, but then watch out.

"I don't know who to trust. I just want that note back," I said, near to tears.

This shook Sally because I am usually pretty calm and rarely show emotions. "It'll be okay. Probably. We just need to catch up with Sammy and avoid contact with Faye until the mystery is solved."

"What if she has it? She'll probably smash my face in as I get off the bus to deliver my papers. What if I have to go to the emergency room with a bloody head wound and can't even see to deliver them? If I live through it, what will people say when I'm all black and blue? I'll have to drop out of school. I won't be able to face everyone. Do I try to fight back or just let her pound on me until she quits? If I tattle on her for doing it, will she finish me off later?" I couldn't stop running all these things through my head. And all of a sudden I couldn't breathe anymore. My heart was pounding so hard that's all I could hear gushing in my own ears.

"Just calm down for now, until we know for sure you are a goner," Sally said, like this was supposed to comfort me.

Science Class, Eighth period

Dear Diary,
Note Crisis:

"Do you want the good news or the bad news?" Sally said as she skidded around the corner and into science class with Sammy following in hot pursuit.

"The note? Did you find it?" I asked.

"Yes, I had it all the time," Sally said, waving the note.

Sammy said, "By the time I had the chance to pass Sally the note without Mrs. Proudfoot seeing, she had gone up to the board too, so I just slipped it into her jacket pocket, and then I guess I forgot to tell her."

I gave Sammy my best "you'll-pay-for-this" glare, and he smiled, hunched his shoulders, and turned both palms up in apology.

I grabbed Sally's arms and squeezed, and we both squealed that the note was in safe hands. Mr. Bookout, our science teacher, motioned for us to take our seats.

"But the bad news is pretty bad," she whispered. "Missy made the mistake of mentioning to Faye Roads that you like Nathan, so she's probably going to kill you anyway."

Home SAFE Home

Dear Diary,

If I want someone to notice me, LIKE NATHAN, I'm invisible. But let me TRY to sneak around invisible in order to avoid a disaster, LIKE FAYE, and I might as well be covered head to toe in Christmas lights with a big old flashing star on top of my head.

"Hey, you."

I kept walking, hoping it was just the wind or my imagination playing tricks on my troubled mind. Or maybe a "Hey, you" for someone else, even though deep down I knew it was the "Hey, you" that, since fifth period, I'd been praying with my whole heart and soul not to hear.

"Hey, Cutright. Turn around!" commanded the voice, just like it was telling a dog to "sit" or "stay."

You can't outrun a voice like that. So I did the only thing I could do. I turned around. Faye was coming up the sidewalk, huffing and puffing, and definitely not smiling.

"Do you have wax in your ears? I've been yelling for two blocks."

"Sorry. I'm late for my paper route," I said, and pointed to my fully loaded bag.

98

"Oh," she said, "then come on," and started walking in the same direction I had been heading. "I heard something a bit distressing today. Missy said you like Nathan. Is this true?"

I swallowed and gulped for air, and I almost walked by Lulu's without leaving a paper. Faye waited while I took a few steps backward and walked up Lulu's steps to put the paper inside the screen door.

"Well, do ya?" she asked. "Like him, I mean?"

"Kind of," I said, and closed my eyes so I wouldn't have to see her fist headed toward my nose.

"Oh," she said, "I figured Missy was making it up, you know, so I'd beat you up. She's tried that before when she gets mad at people, like I'm her hired gun. That gets on my nerves. It might just backfire on Miss Prissy sometime soon. What do you think, should I smash her?"

"I don't know," I said, passing up my chance to get even with Missy. Even though I don't really care much for her, and she never misses an opportunity to stab me in the back, I don't want to see her mangled by the likes of Faye.

"I thought you and Sammy Potter were an item," Faye said, luckily for Missy changing the subject back to my love life.

"What? No way! Who said that?" I said, my face turning bloodred.

"I guess no one when you get right down to it, but you two are together a lot. I think he <u>likes</u> you."

"He just <u>likes</u> to annoy me. He's really good at it." I smiled, surprised to still be alive this far into my conversation with Faye. I'd lived it in my head at least 200,000 times this afternoon, and I was always dead or at least fatally bleeding by the fifth sentence of our exchange.

Faye laughed. "Yeah, he can be annoying, but he's kind of cute, don't you think?"

I just smiled and shrugged my shoulders. I didn't know what response would keep me breathing a little longer, so I played it safe and didn't commit one way or another.

"I'll trade you Nathan for Sammy," she said, just like they were two baseball cards. "Nathan is way too quiet, a real Goody Two-shoes with the teachers. I prefer annoying. Sammy and I are perfect for each other, and we already spend lots of quality time together in detention hall. He makes me laugh." I didn't know anyone could make FAYE laugh. But at that moment, Faye looked just as dreamy-eyed as Gwen does when she talks about Melvin's good traits! Ahhhh.

I didn't know what to say about Faye's proposition. First of all, because I was speechless. I was in shock because it looked like Faye wanted to barter with me instead of murder me. And, second, because I didn't feel that Sammy was exactly mine to trade away. Then I remembered the darned cotton candy he had smeared in my hair last September at the fair for no good reason whatsoever, and heard myself saying, "Deal. He's yours."

"You're not so bad, Cutright," she said. Then she whacked me on the arm (not too hard, but hard ENOUGH), and off she went, as pleased as if I'd given her a million dollars in exchange for a half-eaten, day-old, stepped-on tuna sandwich. I walked home the lightest I had walked in HOURS. Nathan was mine, according to Faye, free and clear. I didn't even have to throw in my bike or my lunch money for next week or anything. Cool.

P.S. Sammy can take care of himself, can't he?

Dear Diary,

I just called the weather station again because I am afraid it may rain out our barbecue and ruin my chances with Nathan. It is supposed to stay warm and sunny. I am glad it is a recording so that the weatherman does not know how often I am calling!

Dear Young and Stylish Magazine Editor,

I don't know if you'll remember me, but I wrote to you about an embarrassing little stroll I took across the gym floor. Well, that's nothing. I've sure topped it for good. For the past couple of weeks, I've been totally obsessed with this guy named, well never mind, but he doesn't even know I exist.

Then something downright amazing happened. Our families decided to get together for a barbecue, so my crush is coming to MY HOUSE tomorrow.

Great, right?

It was, until last night. I was watching TV with my family, and as you can guess, I was COMPLETELY bored out of my mind, so I was playing with this cup of Dr. Pepper, and suctioning it onto my face. I don't know why or how! I must have sucked ALL of the air out or something because the next thing I know, I have this cup STUCK on my face!

Of course I panicked. All my dad said when I ran to him in the kitchen for help was, "What in the world have you done now, goofball?" and then he started laughing. I finally pulled it off with a loud popping sound, which no one could hear but me because everyone was laughing! (Aren't parents supposed to be sympathetic instead of laughing at their children's expense?)

I didn't think any more about it UNTIL this morning, when I woke up with a HUGE CIRCULAR BRUISE AROUND MY MOUTH. The first time I have an opportunity to spend any quality time with the man of my dreams, I've got this giant purple deformity on my face!

Quick, Young and Stylish, what should I do? Do I fake the flu and stay in my room, missing my maybe-once-in-a-life-time chance to get to know my secret crush, or do I tough it out and face him, bruise and all, AND hope I don't cause him to hurl at the picnic table? I can't wait until this comes out in your magazine. Can you write to me today? Anonymous

P.S. Do you think I should bribe my family into not telling this drop-dead gorgeous guy that I'm a dunce who's not even intelligent enough to take a drink without getting the cup vacuumed onto my mouth?

Dear Diary,

Nathan will be here in an hour. After all the cleaning and worrying, now I wish it would rain so hard that they'd have to cancel the barbecue. I don't want anyone to see me!

Mama says to quit acting silly, that no one will even notice the giant bruise on my face. Like anyone could miss it!

"You're not the first person this has ever happened to!" she said. Well, pardon me for disagreeing, but I've never noticed an epidemic of people walking around with cup-size bruises (or drinking glasses) on their mouths!

She won't let me try to cover it up with makeup either. "That will just draw more attention to it," she said and pulled my hands down from my mouth. She just left the room shaking her head. I think she was trying not to laugh.

P.S. She also says I have to come out of my room and be social. Growl. I don't feel like being looked at!

Why me?

Dear Diary,

Gwen and Nathan and their parents are FINALLY here for the barbecue. No one has mentioned my face. Maybe Mama called and warned them how awful I look, so that the Racins wouldn't be too shocked and run screaming.

Nathan looks really good and has on a black T-shirt with #3 NASCAR on it, faded blue jeans, and scruffy-looking tennis shoes. He looks much taller in my yard than he does at school. I wonder why.

I can't help wishing that a TV camera would stop by and tape the whole thing for the world to see. (But then again, I've got this huge bruise on my face. . . . ) I've thought about grabbing the video camera, so I could prove to everyone at school that Nathan Racin was at MY house, but I'm afraid it would just freak him out if I started following him with the camera, and I figure my brothers would burp and say gross things that I wouldn't want anyone at school to see anyway.

Mom grilled hamburgers until the smoke and grease started making her nauseous, and then Dad had to take over, even though he usually burns everything, but by the time everything was ready, none of us would have complained about eating the charcoal on a bun as long as there was plenty of ketchup.

Dad's been doing quite a bit of the cooking lately, especially early in the morning and anything to do with meat frying. If this goes on another four months, he'll probably be better at it than Mama.

Mama said the nausea she's experiencing is a good sign that the baby is a girl because she had lots more morning sickness with me and Katrina than she did with all four boys put together.

Grandma Hanson is trying to tell her that the baby will be a boy because she is carrying it high and round like a basketball, instead of low and oblong like a watermelon. Mama just laughs and says you can't tell by things like that—especially since she's barely showing—but I heard her on the phone the other night telling someone how she spit in Drano the other day, and according to the test, it was going to be a girl for sure. Grown-ups sure can be weird.

I'm afraid Grandma is going to jinx my chances of getting a little sister. She has guessed five out of six of us grandchildren correctly. Actually she doesn't call it <u>guessing</u>. She calls it <u>knowing</u>. She says it comes to her in dreams. I just hope she starts dreaming "GIRL" soon and quits all the talk about boys riding high and basketball-shaped stomachs. I really don't need another brother hanging around here.

I guess Katrina's not really that bad. She's just old. Nineteen. She graduated last year and works full-time at Pizza Hut while she's trying to decide if she wants to go to college for graphic design or if she's going to start studying for her real estate license instead. Plus she goes out on lots of dates because she meets bunches of cute guys at Pizza Hut. I understand that she just doesn't have much time for a twelve-year-old sister. But if Mama has a girl instead of a boy, I vow I'll make PLENTY of time for her. Please let it be a little sister.

Before the barbecue, I wondered what Mama and Daddy would have to talk about with these people from a metropolitan place like Gallipolis, but they seem to have more in common with the Racins than you'd think.

Mr. Racin's a coal miner and so is Dad but in a different mine, so they have lots to talk about. Mrs. Racin is our new postmaster, and although my mom has never worked outside the home, they have found plenty of common ground to talk about too, what with both of them being mothers and daughters and stuff. They started embarrassing all of us by telling stupid things we had done when we were younger.

"I had the hardest time keeping a diaper on Nathan. Every time I turned my back on him, he was stripping and streaking across the yard," said Mrs. Racin, and then she and Mama just cackled and cackled. Nathan turned a hundred shades of red.

"Want to play video games?" I asked.

"Your brothers and I are getting ready to play some ball, but maybe after that. I'm really good. I scored the Master level on Mega-Slime the other day." I had done that three months ago, and I started to say so, but then something stopped me.

"Really?" I said. "That's outrageous. Maybe you can show me your strategy!" I couldn't believe my own ears. I'd seen girls at school giggle and act all dumb as soon as a boy walked into the vicinity, but I never thought that I would fall prey to such a thing.

"Sure, I guess I could give you some pointers," Nathan said, puffing out his chest. "But Mega-Slime is complicated, and I just don't think girls have the motor skills for reaching the Master level," he said, not even realizing that he might have just shortened his life expectancy.

So much for playing the ignorant girl. He is going to lose BIG time as soon as that basketball game is over, and I've just made a few calls to make sure a few of my girlfriends will be present to see his final LOSING score. Tee hee.

Dear Diary,

One thing is for sure. Nathan does not like losing. At first he seemed to enjoy Missy and Sally watching him "teach" me to play, but when I started to win, he said their giggling was breaking his concentration, and that he wasn't feeling well and thought my dad's cooking might have given him food poisoning. Yeah, right. LOSER.

Missy and Sally said they were bored, and so they left once I was so far ahead he could never catch up!

I wonder if he even likes me. He didn't even look at me the whole time he was playing video games. He just stared at the stupid TV screen. Gwen said if a guy likes you, he acts goofy and has trouble talking and blushes a lot. I didn't notice Nathan blushing except when he was mad because I was whipping his pants off at Zoron's Revenge.

Nathan didn't act goofy either. Just boring. Boring and obsessed with conquering Zoron's Revenge. He said he hadn't played that game very much or he could have beaten me, and then went on to brag about how many video games he has because his mom gives him a really big allowance, and he rambled on about his high video scores and spectator sports galore.

I told him I didn't know much about sports, hoping to change the topic to music or TV or movies or something interesting, but I guess he thought my admission of ignorance was a way of begging him for a mini-lecture to catch me up-to-date on the last fifty years of each sport and the statistics on each major athlete for basketball, football, baseball, hockey, NASCAR, bowling, ice fishing, and Frisbee throwing . . . just kidding on the ice fishing and Frisbee throwing. I smiled politely but zoned out after the bowling statistics started.

Maybe he would have been able to talk about something else if we had EVER been left completely alone, but one (or more) of my brothers was always coming in or out and adding to his sports lessons. I think they were encouraging him on purpose just to annoy me.

I thought Nathan would be more interesting, since he's seen different parts of the world other than the Belington Shop-N-Save and the Elkins Wal-Mart and Kmart. But he acts just like most of the other guys at our school.

It's a good thing he has his looks going for him. He is still the most handsome guy in our class, and it would be nice to say he is my boyfriend. I know a few girls who would just eat their hearts out to get to spend time with him. I guess I should thank Melvin for dating Gwen and bringing our families together.

P.S. At the picnic today, Mrs. Racin told me that I'm an attractive girl and that I'm going to look just like Katrina in a couple of years. Katrina smiled at Mrs. Racin. I looked over at Katrina, and I twisted up my face and said, "Ah no, anything but that." I'm not sure why I said such a thing, but I think it's just my way of dealing with a compliment. Deep down it was a good feeling because Katrina is EXTREMELY pretty, and no one has ever said anything like that to me before.

I wonder if I am good-looking? Or did Mrs. Racin just feel sorry for my bruise?

NATHAN didn't even seem to notice that I had my best Backstreet Boys T-shirt and new bibs on. (But then again, he didn't mention the bruise either!)

Mrs. Racin is really nice. Too bad her son can't play video games worth diddly.

**From:** "Venola"<cutright1@mtnbelle.net>
**To:** "Gwendolyn"<racins@mtnbelle.net>
**Subject: To Face or Not to Face**
**Date:** Sunday, March 26; Time: 22:15

Dear Gwen,
  I think everyone at school will laugh at my ugly bruised face tomorrow. You are the smartest person I know. What should I do? How can I get my parents to let me stay home?
  Is there any makeup strong enough to cover it?
Desperately yours,
Venola (bag-over-her-head?) Cutright

Monday, March 27

Homeroom

Dear Diary,

I think Gwen's advice worked. I walked into homeroom and made a huge joke about the cup getting stuck on my face, and said that after this klutzy incident, Dad told me never ever to touch the super glue. Everyone laughed but then went back to finishing their homework. Something tells me EVERYONE goofed off this weekend, not just ME. I think we are all suffering from spring fever and are sick of schoolwork.

Dear Gwen,

I followed your advice, and it was perfect! The only person who said anything was this guy named Sammy. When he ran over and opened my chocolate milk at lunch, he said, "Be careful now. We don't want to have to call 911." Just between us, it was kind of fun to get the extra attention. Just so they don't put my picture in the yearbook as "Most Likely to Get a Cup Stuck on Her Face"!

Thanks again for being my friend! Melvin is a lucky guy!

Love,
Vennie

Dear Diary,

Well, Gwen helped me get over the embarrassment of the bruise on my face, but after today, my face won't be the only place I have a bruise. Oh, my aching feet! We started square-dancing week in gym class. One week every year Mr. Fenstermacher decides that we need some kind of cultural activity other than the day-in/day-out death stinger ball (kind of like dodgeball, but only vicious coed–junior high style that leaves us girls with big red sting marks on our legs). Who knows, maybe there's some strange objective that Mr. Fenstermacher is forced to meet: "Students must be forced to do-si-do."

Mr. Fenstermacher's brother is our town's pediatrician, who just happens to call out square dancing on weekends, so our teacher asks Dr. Fenstermacher in, and Dr. Fenstermacher obliges by closing down his office and coming over and singing weird verses to us like, "All join hands and roll that wheel, the more you dance, the better you'll feel!"

He barks out these strange commands that make no sense whatsoever like "swing and promenade"

or "grand right and left" or "couples circulate."
Then we have to try and follow and pretend like
we're having a good time because most of us are
beholden to Dr. Fenstermacher because he's
responsible for bringing us into this world. Not
to mention that if we don't conform, he'll tell our
parents we misbehaved during his dance week the
next time we have a doctor's appointment. Or
maybe he won't be so gentle when it is shot time!

The real name for square dancing should be
"torture to annoyingly irritating music." Since
Mr. Fenstermacher forces all the boys to participate,
they've come up with a plan that makes it as
dangerous as death stinger ball. The boys approach
us like it's some kind of primal battlefield, and pass
us back and forth with such velocity that some girls
come near to passing out, but others of us have
learned to stomp toes with the best of the guys,
and so it's pretty much a free-for-all by the time
Dr. Fenstermacher tells us to bow and curtsy to
our partners and hit the showers. More than one
on each side usually leaves the battlefield limping.

Sally always claims to be too sick to participate,
but not me. The last couple years I've gotten pretty
good at getting even on the toe smashing, but this
year I was happy when the whole thing was over,
because the guys are getting bigger and lifting

weights, and Nathan and Tommy and Jason and EVEN SAMMY acted like we were playing bumper cars instead of dancing. I can't wait to get back to something less cultural and much safer like a nice friendly game of death stinger ball.

P.S. No one has called me Boom-da-dee-boom for a while! Life is good.

S.,

If my parents let me go on the trip to Washington, D.C., will you sit with me, or are you going to hang out with A.J.? I think Mrs. Proudfoot will let us sit together if we promise not to giggle too loud.

Mama isn't going to chaperone because she can't stand on her feet very long, now that she's pregnant. She ALWAYS volunteers as a chaperone. If she lets me go, this will be my first time out of town alone. Mama is in the "we'll see" stage. Is your mother going?

V.

**From:** "Venola"<cutright1@mtnbelle.net>
**To:** "Sally"<scathell@mtnbelle.net>
**Subject: Operation Wear Down**
**Date:** Saturday, April 1; Time: 16:29


Dear S.,
  Guess what? My parents have decided
I can go, as long as I "find work and
promise to send lots of money home." Dad
is a real comedian sometimes.
  So are we going to sit together?
Ven

P.S. My parents better not be playing an
April Fools' Day joke!

Blessed Easter Egg Extravaganza

Dear Diary,

Now that Faye isn't an immediate danger (Faye is always a looming danger), I thought today was going to be perfect. Finally Nathan and I were going to get a chance to spend some time alone together, away from my house full of brothers and ESPN and video games. I'd get a chance to find out his other interests and what we have in common and stuff.

Both my family and the Racins went to the sunrise service, which was followed by a buckwheat pancake breakfast, a special Easter performance by the choir, and an Easter egg hunt at noon for kids one to sixteen.

At first, Bobby said he is fourteen and way too old to look for stupid Easter eggs, but when he found out the prize for the most eggs was a new mountain bike, he and his two best friends slept over and stayed up, planning strategies for covering the most area per minute. They wanted to commando the church grounds and take turns standing guard. They had their binoculars, sleeping bags, and stuff ready to go watch the church elders hide the eggs, but Mama got wise to their plan somehow (tee hee) and shamed them for trying to cheat on something so sacred as an Easter bike. They were ordered not to leave the yard without her permission. But they went on with their planning until at least one in the morning, when I finally passed out.

Gwen said Nathan and I could ride to the church with her and Melvin, and I was ready extra early because I figured if I were a minute late getting dressed Melvin would sneak off in his old Camaro without me, even though I helped him wash and wax it yesterday.

When we pulled up at Gwen's house, I climbed into the back and Nathan crawled in beside me. There isn't much floor space in those sports cars anyway, but when your brother doesn't want you along, he has a tendency to shove the seat ALL the way back, so Nathan's and my legs couldn't help but brush up against one another as we sat there with our knees poking up to our chins.

We both mumbled a "hi," but none of us were awake enough to make any real conversation or crack any good jokes or anything.

Nathan and I decided to help with breakfast, instead of just standing around looking stupid waiting for the Easter egg hunt to begin. He was in charge of keeping butter on the tables, and I got syrup duty (which was a stickier situation. Ha. Ha.).

Sammy was around too, and he cleaned up after lazy people who left their plates on the table. He pretended to be stuck to the floor in an ooey-gooey syrupy spot. Reverend Lawson caught us laughing at him and yelled at Sammy for getting the syrup all over his feet, like he meant to step in it, and said, "You would have tracked that stuff upstairs all over the church's new carpet, if I hadn't caught you. Boy, are you possessed? Take off those shoes and wash them good, and you two quit giggling and help him clean up the floor here." Sammy can get under people's skin wherever he goes, and he usually drags others into trouble too. I should know better than to hang out with him after all these years.

Next came the egg hunt. By the time it officially started, the sun was baking down on us, and I felt like a syrup-covered slug. It probably didn't help matters that I'd eaten about three and a half plain pancakes and two buckwheat ones. I was ready to curl up in the shade on a picnic bench for a starch-induced nap instead of racing around a churchyard looking for food that I wouldn't eat if I were stranded on a deserted island. (I don't particularly like eggs, because of where they come from AND because they are slimy, but I especially don't want anything to do with eggs that have food coloring seeping into the white jiggly part and that have been out in the hot sun for hours.)

I thought the hunt would be broken up into categories according to age, but instead they gave us each a little decorated bucket made out of a two-liter pop bottle. Then Reverend Lawson blew his official referee whistle (he does that at basketball games during the week), and off everyone went. Bobby and his crew took off like Rangers combing a minefield. They acted like none of them had ever owned a bike before in their lives. I don't even think they stopped to question how they would all share it if they won.

Maybe if I hadn't just bought a new bike with my paper route money, I'd have cared more about winning, but I'm not so sure. Everyone scrambling around looked kind of pathetic, and like I said, I was just too full of pancakes to do much. After the laughs with Sammy and Nathan in the basement, I got brave enough to ask Nathan if he wanted to search together. "You gotta be kidding. Share a bike with a girl?" and off he took like a chicken with his head cut off.

Well, I just stood there stunned, because Nathan had said "GIRL" like it was a diseased word. Jilted again. I looked for Sally, but she wasn't even searching for eggs. She and A.J. were walking around the gravestones holding hands, and Karla and Jason were sitting under a tree. Missy goes to a different church, so she wasn't even there to talk to.

That's when I saw Sammy. No longer glued to the floor, he was out in the field entertaining some toddlers with cartwheels and magic tricks. My pretty little blond neighbor girl Anna Marie had tears and mucus running down her face because almost everybody had an egg but her. Sammy pulled a sparkly pink one with purple flowers out from behind her ear, and the little girl's laughter gurgled up from deep inside. Anna Marie probably needs to laugh because I hear her parents arguing at the top of their lungs all the time when I'm delivering their paper.

As far back as I can remember, I've only seen my mama and daddy have one real argument. I was only seven, and I just remember being really scared, and going to bed thinking that my parents were going to get a divorce, and I would have to choose which parent I was going to live with, and I didn't want to make either one mad or sad, and that maybe I would just go live with Grandma and Grandpa Hanson because they always had a refrigerator full of orange pop and a box of Vanilla Wafers squirreled away in the second cabinet from the left. Then the next day the argument was over, and Daddy brought flowers home for Mama.

I watched Sammy for a couple of minutes. Every time he found an egg, he looked around for a little kid who wasn't doing very well alone.

I caught up with him and said, "You're never going to win that way."

He shrugged and grinned sheepishly. "What would I do with a new bike besides wreck it?" he asked.

126

"The one I have now is broken in the way I want it."

So I helped him, and I felt like Robin Hood. Once I thought I was going to have to tackle Nathan and Bobby, who went for the same egg as Sammy under a fence post, but they backed off when they saw we meant business. Anna Marie at least ended the day with two eggs! She was smiling ear to ear, and blew Sammy the sweetest kiss that would make the hardest heart in the world ache for another. I wish Mama could have a baby that acts just like Anna Marie. I could get used to having her around really fast.

P.S. I hope Faye doesn't think I was flirting with her guy!

P.P.S. Bobby's team didn't win! Some nine-year-old girl did. She must have been psychic, because she found that pile of eggs so fast.

Dear S.,
   Am I all packed? Yeah, right. I've
changed what I'm taking a hundred times.
All of my clothes are back out on the
floor and bed and dresser just like old
times. How long ago was it that I cleaned
my room? You couldn't tell now!
   Just think, tomorrow night, we'll be in
a big city with no parents.
   I guess it is too bad that we've got
assigned seats, and that we're not near
the guys, but I'm REALLY glad Mrs.
Proudfoot let us sign up together. I'm
not sure I could find enough to talk
about with Nathan all the way to D.C. Or
what if I got sick and threw up on him?
Too excited to sleep,
V.

**From:** "Venola"<cutright1@mtnbelle.net>
**To:** "Sally"<scathell@mtnbelle.net>
**Subject: No Hurling Allowed**
**Date:** Monday, April 10; Time: 20:43


Dear Sally,
  Do you think we'll all have to stay in
a big group or will we have free time to
explore?
  Maybe we'll see the President or the
First Lady or someone famous at the
White House.
Vennie

P.S. No, I'm not going to throw up on
you!

Dear Diary,

Guess what? Mrs. Proudfoot assigned Missy and Karla to room with Sally and me. She thought we would be pleased to be with our "friends." I guess I should be glad not to be with someone we don't know very well, but the two have been talking for weeks about all the things they plan to get into. Oh boy.

I'm not a super wimp, but I don't want to get into trouble!

Dear Diary,

I am SO tired. We have nicknamed our bus tour guide Ms. Hitler because she has been herding us in and out of all kinds of places. We stepped inside this neat train station–shopping place called Union Station, but just about the time everyone got off the bus, ate at McDonald's, and walked around a little, Ms. Hitler was yelling for us to line up because we were behind schedule for the National Aquarium and the Capitol tour. I didn't even have time to go into Claire's, and I love that store!

I thought the National Aquarium was really cool, even though Missy kept yawning and complaining that the one in Baltimore, Maryland, is much newer and better. Hey, all I've got to say is this one is better than our local fish hatchery, and that's the only place I've ever been up close to fish before. I'd liked to have spent the whole day watching the fish, but we just spent an hour.

I took notes on all the different kinds of sharks, and where they can be found. If I'm going to scuba dive with sharks, I figure I should learn as much about them as possible. My favorites are the lemon and the nurse sharks, but the leopard one was cool too. Sammy got into trouble for pecking on their tanks. He said he was just being friendly, but I wonder how he would feel if pedestrians kept pecking on his window as we inched along in traffic today.

In the Capitol building, there were so many other groups roaming around, it was hard to stay focused on what our Capitol guide was saying. That's when I saw HER, a girl painted in the top of the rotunda who looks just like me. It's a really weird painting of George Washington being lifted into the sky by thirteen angelic-looking maidens (which the guide said represented the original colonies).

I was so spooked by seeing myself painted on the ceiling that I did something I shouldn't have. I moved to the front of the group and actually raised my hand to ask a question—which next to barfing is about the most uncool and embarrassing thing you can do when you are in seventh grade and on a school field trip.

"Who's the girl, the one with the shield and sword?" I heard myself asking.

The guide, apparently thrown off by a junior high student showing a spark of interest, said, "Uh, that's Freedom, triumphing over Tyranny and Kingly Power." From that moment I was caught like a deer in the headlights. He went on for five minutes, telling me about how the fresco was recently cleaned, the process for its cleaning, when it was painted originally, and that the painter, a guy named Brumidi, had dedicated his life to making "our" (the guide acted like he meant just mine and his) Capitol beautiful and deserving enough for a country based on liberty.

(Note to self: NEVER EVER make eye contact with a tour guide. It's worse than being the teacher's pet!)

P.S. Now I'm in a daze, wondering if my twin "Freedom" is some kind of sign. Maybe it's my destiny to do something great, like run for Congress, or become President. Should I? Senator Byrd talked to our group and told us that he was raised in impoverished circumstances during the Great Depression. He said if he did it, we can too if we work hard. I wonder how hard he is talking? Study-with-the-radio-on hard, or never-see-TV-again hard? P.P.S. I picked up a brochure on becoming a page. Imagine, ME, Venola Mae Cutright, running errands and taking messages for important politicians! I can't do it until I'm fourteen, but at least I'm allowed then! Before 1971, girls weren't even allowed to apply! So if I'm meant to be President, this page thing might be the way to go. I'd have to go to a special school in the Library of Congress, and it would probably be really hard work, like Senator Byrd said, but at least I wouldn't have to share a room with a B-A-B-Y! Wonder if Sally would do it too?

3:15 P.M.

Dear Diary,

Boy, were we disappointed this morning! It said
on our itinerary that we were going to spend some
free time at the Mall. No one told us that's what
they call the downtown area where the museums
and monuments are located!

But even though it wasn't a shopping mall, we
did see some impressive things. One of the most
unforgettable places was the Vietnam Veterans
Memorial. At first, I didn't see anything special, and
Sally and I were just talking about the new kind of
fingernail polish that looks like it has cracks running
all over your nails and whether Missy had been
flirting with "our" guys on the bus, but then IT was
just THERE, all of a sudden, this black granite V
with over 58,000 names of those killed or missing
in Vietnam. Some people were tracing names on
slips of paper I thought about looking for Cutrights
to see if anyone shared the name of my brothers or
dad, but I thought it might be bad luck.

People were walking around crying, even grown

men, which I had never seen before in public. I thought some of the class clowns might say something smart or yell something disgusting, but everyone was quiet, even after we got back on the bus.

The same thing happened at the Tomb of the Unknown Soldier. We watched the changing of the guards, and no one whispered or complained about being hot or elbowed the person next to him or anything.

But on the way back to the hotel it was a different story. It was almost a riot. The guide pointed out the biggest shopping mall I've ever seen, which was a mistake, because then she wouldn't stop the bus, so lots of kids were really angry and complaining about just looking at tombstones and statues and buildings all day, when they had been promised a mall. Some booed the guide until Mrs. Proudfoot made them be quiet.

4:45 P.M.

Dear Diary,

Trouble is brewing. Missy and Karla are totally outraged because Ms. Hitler wouldn't stop at that dynamite mall, and they are muttering all kinds of things about constitutional rights. They are determined to get there THIS EVENING.

After supper we have free time from six to nine P.M. to rest in our rooms, play video games in the hotel arcade, and swim in the pool, but we are UNDER NO CIRCUMSTANCES ALLOWED TO LEAVE THE PREMISES.

Sally says she wants to go with them, that it might be her only chance to step foot in a REAL mall, and she thinks that as her friend, I should go too. Am I letting her down? I just don't WANT to do this!!!

First, I don't like to lie. I'd feel guilty the whole time, and if we got murdered or came up missing, I wouldn't want to get the chaperones or teachers in trouble, even though I'm not doing too well in Mrs. Proudfoot's class. And Missy's and Karla's moms are chaperones, so the teachers might not yell at them too much for sneaking out, but I know my parents would <u>kill</u> me. At first, Mama didn't even want to let me go on the trip at all, but I told her, now that I wasn't going to be the baby anymore, I hoped that she would trust me to make good decisions. (This new baby might work out to my advantage.)

Second, even if I wanted to skip out to the mall, which part of me does, I wouldn't want to go with Missy and Karla. I don't trust their sticky fingers.

What can I do while they are gone? I can't swim, so I'm definitely not going to let Nathan see me wading around the shallow part with the little kids. Maybe I can get Sammy and Faye to let me play video games with them, but then again, I better not. They might ask about my roommates, and I'm not that great of a liar. Guess I'll just hang out in the room until they get back. Then I can listen to their adventures for the rest of the evening. Yahoo!

Thursday, April 13

Dear Diary,

They are gone. They called a taxi from the room, and I just watched them get in. Yikes!

7:45 P.M.

Dear Diary,

Honest, I didn't tell! Missy's mom knocked on our door not even an hour after they left, and she asked where Missy and the other two were.

"Down at the pool," I said, like I was supposed to if anyone asked.

"No, they aren't. And they aren't playing videos either." Then she looked me dead in the eye and asked, "Did they go to the mall?"

I didn't say anything. I didn't shrug my shoulders, or mumble an "I don't know." I just stood there.

"I knew it," she said. "I should have known that headstrong girl wasn't going to take no for an answer. Missy begged me all through supper, and when she knew I meant business, she just smiled and walked away."

Oh boy.

So Mrs. Fowler dragged me down to the pool to be grilled by Mrs. Proudfoot, while she and Karla's mom hotfooted it to the mall.

7:55 A.M.

Dear Diary,

What's worse than not getting to see the mall with your friends? Having them come back not talking to you because they think you ratted on them, and you STILL have to spend the night in the same room. To show that they really hate me, they are completely ignoring me. Sally went to bed, turned over against the wall, and pretended to be asleep.

I tried asking what happened, and no one said anything. But I've pretty much figured it out because Karla and Missy spent most of the night talking about it.

Moms must have radar. They didn't even have to go into the mall. The girls were standing at the bus stop out front. It turns out that taxis cost more than the three thought, and they were ripped off to boot. The driver said, "Twelve dollars and fifty cents," but none of them had the right change. So Sally and Karla each gave him their ONLY ten-dollar bill, expecting change, and the driver took off with a big tip. After splitting the price of the taxi, none of the girls had much money to spend in the mall or enough for a taxi ride back. So they spent most of their mall time finding out how to take a bus to the hotel.

They act as if I'm a traitor for not being in trouble with them. Should I have gone? If I'm really supposed to be like the Freedom girl with the shield, don't I have to stand up for what I believe in, even if it is uncool?

Seventh grade stinks.

2:30 P.M.


Dear Diary,

Washington, D.C., is no fun by yourself. Our tour group zoomed through some art and history museums, but besides some really cool giant Madagascar hissing cockroaches at the live insect exhibit in the Museum of Natural History, I don't remember much of what I saw because my ex-friends, who have to stay right next to Mrs. Proudfoot, keep giving me dirty looks. Sally just stares at the ground. All the other kids probably think I'm a tattletale too.

I haven't seen Nathan. He went with a different group to the sports museum and the National Zoo. We're all supposed to meet later at the National Air and Space Museum for a planetarium show. At least it will be dark there, and no one will be able to see that I'm alone.

4:00 P.M.

Dear Diary,

The planetarium would have been really neat if I could have concentrated, but not much matters when your best friend hates you. At the end of the presentation, the guide turned on the lights and asked, "What is our place in the universe?"

How am I supposed to know about the universe? I don't even know what my place is in seventh-grade romances, or on a field trip, or a school bus. Even at home, my place in the family is changing. Ugh. Why couldn't the guide just show us the stars and leave it at that?

9:00 P.M.

Dear Diary,

The bus ride home was fantastic after all. On the way out of the planetarium, Sally motioned to me and said, "I need to talk to you."

I walked over to where she stood, still in confinement with Mrs. Proudfoot. "I owe you an apology. Mrs. Proudfoot told me you didn't squeal. Sorry I didn't believe you last night. I was just mad."

Maybe I should have been angry and just walked away, but you don't do that to a real friend. So I just shrugged and said, "It's okay. Sorry that you didn't get to go shopping."

"That was probably the best thing that could have happened," she said. "I'll tell you the WHOLE story later. Will you see if you can sit up front with me on the bus? I'm not allowed back at our assigned seat."

And so I did sit up front. Sally told me how the whole way to the mall, Missy and Karla whispered about how they were going to steal more expensive things such as lingerie and perfume, since they were out of town, and she told me when she said she wasn't going to help, they called her some names and made fun of her. They even called her a "VENOLA." She was scared that she was either going to have to find her way back to the hotel by herself, or get caught with the shoplifters. So she was glad when the taxi driver took most of their money, and they had to give up their shopping plans to find the bus.

It turns out she wasn't just mad at me last night for turning them in. She was mad at herself for being stupid enough to go with Karla and Missy. She said she wanted to talk to me all day, but Mrs. Proudfoot pretty much had her handcuffed to her like a dangerous criminal so that she wouldn't get away or steal a painting or anything.

Dear Diary,

I should have known! Right when I get my best friend back, something happens and I lose her.

I called Sally just now, and Mrs. Cathell answered the phone and said that Sally is grounded and has lost phone privileges for a WHOLE week.

Stupid me had to go and ask if we could still E-mail each other, and she said, "Thanks for mentioning that, Venola. I hadn't even thought about restricting computer usage." Now we can't do that either. Me and my big, fat mouth!

Mama says she is proud of me for not sneaking out to the mall. She says the others acted immaturely, and that in addition to endangering themselves, the girls have endangered future trips to D.C. She said, "The board of education is always looking for a reason to cut these cultural things out of the budget."

I hope they don't. I sure wouldn't want my future little sister to miss out on the experience of an overnight field trip. You haven't lived until you've survived one!

**From:** "Venola"<cutright1@mtnbelle.net>
**To:** "Sally"<scathell@mtnbelle.net>
**Subject: Home Sweet Home**
**Date:** Sunday, April 16; Time: 08:13

Dear Sally,
  It's good to be home, isn't it? Or maybe
not, since you are grounded. Sorry! :-(
  I hope your mom lets you check your
E-mail soon.
  I just wanted to make sure you had E-
mail when you were finally back on-line
AND to let you know that I've been
invited to Nathan's house. Well, not
exactly by Nathan, but he's going to be
there. Gwen says she wants me to come to
supper too, and Nathan has agreed to a
rematch of Zoron's Revenge.
  I won't write a lot because we'll probably be able to talk details at school
before you are allowed to check your E-
mail. I hope you aren't suffering too
bad from net withdrawals.
Missing you,
Vennie

P.S. Katrina is talking about getting an
apartment with a girl she works with at
Pizza Hut, so if that happens, I can have
her room and the baby can have my cracker
box! Life is looking up!
P.P.S. Do you think it's wrong to annoy
Katrina more than usual just to help her
make up her mind? :-)

Dear Diary,

Gwen was sitting in the porch swing when Melvin and I pulled up at her house. "Nathan's down at the pond. Why don't you go see if he's caught anything?" Gwen said and winked. I think she's finally on to all my questions about him.

I would have just as soon stayed and talked with Gwen, but Melvin sat down beside her in the swing and motioned for me to move along. Brothers are jerks.

So what could I do but move along? I'm smart enough to know when I'm not wanted.

My hair was a mess after riding in Melvin's stupid car at a zillion miles an hour with the windows down. As I walked around the corner of the house, I straightened my hair in the reflection of one of the windows, but it's hard to do much by just running my fingers through the tangles.

I didn't see Nathan until I was all the way down at the pond. But once I saw him, I knew why he was sitting kind of hidden in the tall grass.

"How long have you been doing that?" I asked.

Nathan took another drag on his cigarette and smiled. "Want to try it?"

I shook my head no. My grandmother and grandfather Hanson have always smoked, and it is one of the few things I would like to change about them. I hate the smell that lingers on their clothes and books and on the things they give me—even weeks after I take them home with me, they still smell bad. For my tenth birthday, Grandma made me a beautiful <u>Gone with the Wind</u> doll cake, and she stuck a real Barbie doll in the middle of a cake shaped like a southern hoop dress, and she decorated it in blue and white frosting. She even crocheted a little blue-and-white Scarlett O'Hara hat for Barbie's head. I fell in love with the darned thing, but when we finally cut it at suppertime, it tasted like ashes. Yuck. I vowed never to smoke a cigarette and had to spit the cake out in my napkin when no one was looking.

Nathan didn't want to take my simple refusal of his cigarette as an answer. "Come on. Are you chicken? Afraid you'll puke? Afraid you'll get in trouble?" he crooned.

Before I could explain why I'd never even consider smoking, he threw the cigarette in the pond, grabbed his fishing pole, and started waving the other hand around in the air, like he was being chased by giant mosquitoes. Mrs. Racin was walking toward us with a big plate of cookies.

So much for Mr. Big Shot.

P.S. Did I mention that smoking must kill video game skills? I creamed him. Tee hee.

P.P.S. It must also deaden any sense of humor. He didn't think it was funny when I teased him about a girl "without" motor skills making it to the Master level.

P.P.P.S. I challenged him to a bike race too. But he refused to race "a girl." Scaredy-cat!

Dear Diary,

Okay, according to my new buddy Faye, Nathan is mine.

There's just one problem. I'm not sure I want him. Lately I'm not so sure Nathan is my Mr. Perfect anymore. All he cares about is sports and video game scores. Plus after the whole Easter egg thing, he seems kind of sexist and selfish. I think maybe I was caught up in the excitement of having a MASH option outside of Belington's boring choices of A.J., Sammy Potter, and Glue-Eating Boy.

Tuesday, April 18

Dear Diary,

Could it be that I just wanted to be IN LOVE, and that was more important than the WHO?

I asked Gwen how you know if you are in love, and she said, "Your cheeks get hot, and you have trouble concentrating on anything but that other person." It is hard to believe that she feels this way about my gross, Neanderthal brother.

I figured if Mama was willing to have six of my dad's children, and another on the way, she might know something about true love, so I decided to ask her too.

"You know right away," she said. "You want to be with him every minute of the day, and when you finally get a chance to talk, everything that person says sounds like your own thoughts echoing back." I'm not sure I want to be with ANYONE every single minute of every single day, and I know I don't want anyone's thoughts echoing back just like mine. That would be just plain weird and annoying.

But it sure would have been nice to give Karla and Jason a run for cutest couple in the yearbook.

153

Honestly though, Nathan and I don't fit any of these guidelines. My cheeks usually don't heat up unless I'm getting yelled at by a teacher, which is more often than you'd think, and Nathan and I don't seem to have very much in common at all. On club day, he joined 4-H and chess, while I joined chorus and Future Teachers of America. I figured a guy from a place with a strange, beautiful name like Gallipolis would want to be a diamond thief or at least an international spy or a writer of books like Gulliver's Travels.

The two of us never have really talked. He never says much to any of us girls. He is good at sports and is always chosen for basketball at lunchtime, which doesn't allow him much time for teasing and flirting with us. Guess a guy has to choose priorities. Sammy Potter would much rather run around pecking on girls' shoulders and pointing to the next person, or dropping ice down our blouses than playing basketball. Too bad Nathan isn't more like Sammy. . . .

Dear Diary,

Well I've filled all your pages, and I didn't find the man of my dreams, but I'm still glad I bought you, Diary, instead of a pair of jeans—especially since I'm growing so fast that the jeans would probably be too short by now!

I think I did accomplish my main goal for the spring. Didn't I ask you for some exciting and heart-wrenching times? What could be as exciting as coming face-to-face with the likes of Faye AND SURVIVING! (And finding that she's kind of nice.) Or what could be as heart-wrenching as almost losing your best friend? Plus, there's my parents' big news. They are determined to help me not be the baby of the family, and are even going to the trouble of having ANOTHER BABY to do so. (Just kidding. Having a kid SISTER around might be neat. Maybe I can help her avoid some of my mistakes—boom-da-dee-boom, ahhhh! Did I really do that?) And I guess there's still time for learning to rock climb, to scuba dive peacefully with sharks, and to play the bongos with aborigines in some far,

far distant land from Belington before letting a game of MASH or the scientific technique of Love/Marriage/Hate/Divorce cast my future with a boy in stone!

Until then, stay cool, but don't freeze to death! Signing off,
Venola Mae Cutright (aka Freedom),
Future Page and President